Watching Her Sleep

K. A. Moore

Published by K. A. Moore, 2019.

Book cover design by Betibup33 design

Edited by Jessica at Bookhelpline

ISBN 9781733236201 (ebook)

ISBN 9781957223124 (paperback)

Also by K. A. Moore

Relics Series

Relics

The Key

The Chosen

Standalone

Watching Her Sleep

Sentinel

Weeping Widow's Heirloom

In memory of some of the best officers I'vehad the honor and privilege of working with.Officers Hurt #0113 Orr #1502 & Rath #0710

One

"NO, I'M SURE! WHY WON'T you believe me? There was someone in my house!" Kassidy Parker's frustration boiled over at the officer they sent when she called the local police department several minutes earlier. It felt as if she were talking to a brick wall.

"Ma'am we wanna make sure. We've been through your house. There're no signs of forced entry. Are you sure no one has a key? Could you have left a door unlocked?" The officer peered down at her.

Kassidy clenched her fists. "I never use my front door so it's never unlocked. The back door was locked when I got home because I had to unlock it to go out to start the grill. No, no one has a key to my house or a garage door opener! Does that cover it?"

"Well, we can definitely put that in your statement. Is it possible you put the dishes out before you left?"

"No. You even said there are no fingerprints on the dishes, correct?" The deep breath she had taken in rushed out as she counted to ten.

"No, there are no fingerprints on the dishes."

Kassidy raised an eyebrow with a question to the young officer. "So, do you have a habit of wiping your fingerprints off of your own dishes you get out of the cabinet to use for your dinner?"

Pen poised over his notebook, an apparent light bulb went off in his head. "Well, no. I don't."

"Well, neither do I!" She glared at him and hoped the common sense of the situation would kick in so he would know someone had been in her house.

"I see yer point. Is there anything else you noticed, besides the dishes?"

"No, but they put out the exact dishes I would've myself with what I planned to make for dinner. I think someone's watching me." She turned her back to the officer and stared at the island in the kitchen. The dishes were perfectly set out for steak, salad, and corn on the cob right down to the corncob skewers she kept in the back of the drawer.

"What we can do is have an officer step up patrols in your area. Okay with you?"

The officer diligently wrote as she turned around to face him.

"Can I get my report number for this crime?" Kassidy fumed at the officer's apparent disinterest in her case.

"Well, ma'am, since we can't find any signs of forced entry and no evidence that someone was in here, we can't prove a crime occurred. You even said nothing's missing. In situations like this, the detective that would be assigned has nothing to go on and would just close out the case."

"Oh yes, there was a crime! I didn't give anyone permission to be in my house, much less set the table for me!"

"I'm sorry but there's nothing to suggest someone was in here."

Kassidy gestured toward the perfectly placed dishes for her meal. "There's your evidence right there. Correct?"

"Yes, but - "

Kassidy held up a hand before he could say anything else. Did he not want to write a report? How else could she get through to him that someone had been in her house? "Then you need to file this as a burglary because I'm telling you someone came into my house without my permission. I don't care if I left the front door wide open. I didn't give anyone the authority to come into my house today. I'm sorry to say this, but maybe we need your supervisor to come out so I can discuss this with them."

"No, ma'am." Mic in hand, the officer spoke with dispatch for a report number that he scratched on his business card. "We'll have a detective follow up with you in a few days."

"Thank you, and there really was someone in my house." Kassidy took the card the officer held out for her. She ran her fingers over the smooth surface and felt the indents where he had written the case number.

The deadbolt sounded softly as she locked the door. The officer lumbered down the steps from her deck. Anxious, she gathered up all the dishes then dumped them in the sink. She yanked on the stuck refrigerator door and the coolness of the interior hit her as it rocketed open. The food hit the cavernous bottom of the trashcan with a thud. Did he put something in her food? Images of her lying on the cold tiled kitchen floor filled her head. Her stomach growled and jerked her back to reality. She placed a quick order for Chinese food. The thought of pork fried rice made her mouth water.

Her eyes darted everywhere, half expecting someone to be lurking around every corner. She jumped as she passed a coat slung over the back of a dining room chair. She shuffled from room to room. Every corner seemed darker than normal as if it held an ominous being ready to grab her. Routine was her security blanket. She knew where everything belonged and everything had its place in her house, but something still felt off. She couldn't put a finger on why. Maybe it was the knowledge that someone had invaded the sanctuary and privacy of her home. Shivers ran down her back as goosebumps covered her skin. Was someone watching her now? Would she know if they were?

Darkness ebbed into her house as she closed all the blinds and curtains, certain she was being watched. It didn't ease her suspicions when she had them all closed but only made the darkness more menacing. The doorbell rang and ripped her from her wild imagination. With wallet in hand, she marched up to the back door. She opened the door and her heart dropped, there was no one there. Ten seconds later, she saw the delivery driver pull into her driveway.

Kassidy forced a smile and gave a generous tip to the driver. With the door closed and locked behind her, she was no longer hungry for the food she'd ordered, which smelled delicious. Growls from her stomach convinced her to eat, even though nausea from the day's events hit her stomach like a ton of bricks. Light bounced off the ceramic glaze of the dishes in the sink, catching her eye. It was a reminder of what could have happened if someone had drugged her food.

Dread filled her at the thought of going to bed. Would they get in again while she slept? The cold steel of the locks chilled her fingers as she double- and then triple-checked them all. After she turned off the lights, she crossed into the dark shadows of the hallway and crept to her room. She closed and locked the bedroom door, for the first time since she had moved in, barring anyone from entering her room.

With the bathroom light turned off, she crawled under the heavy weight of the covers. She couldn't fall asleep to save her life. Hours passed by as she tossed and turned. The weight of the blankets that used to be a warm, welcoming safe place, were now restrictive and suffocating. Finally, sleep took control as she drifted off.

Awakened with a start, she lay there paralyzed, gripped by fear. Sure that something clattered from down the hall, she listened for several agonizing minutes before sleep tore her from consciousness. Roused from her sleep yet again, sure that something moved in the kitchen, her palms started to sweat as she waited for confirmation that she had heard something.

At five o'clock, she admitted defeat: there was no way she was getting any reasonable amount of sleep, so she got up for the day. The tea kettle whistled to announce that the water was boiling, as steam vented out of the spout. With tea in hand she kicked her feet up on the chair across from her on the deck. The watercolor painting in the sky showed shades of pinks and reds that swirled in the clouds as the sun peeked on the horizon. She thanked God for His beautiful artwork and sat in awe.

The rising sun on a new day made the fear and dread from the previous night ebb away. Panic seemed to be on a vacation, instead of lying in wait to seize her in her calm quiet home. The first chore on her list today was a trip to the grocery store and to run errands. A good run first would help clear her head.

Her cup joined the other dishes in the sink from the previous night. After she changed her clothes, she slid on her running shoes. The end of her ponytail swept back and forth across her shoulder blades as she strolled to the back door. Kassidy placed her phone securely in its running case then fastened it around her lean arm. She hit play then put in her earbuds as the music filled her head with words of worship.

The music drowned out her scare from yesterday. She found her stride and took off. When she ran, she could clear her head and talk to God. There was nothing He couldn't handle. He was a best friend you could talk to no matter what. He was the only one who could handle anything she had. She would lay all her concerns at His feet and know they couldn't be in better hands.

On the second lap around, neighbors woke up and waved sleepily as their slippered feet shuffled down the cold porous concrete for their morning papers. The close-knit small town she lived in made her feel as if she were a part of a large family. Everyone was friendly and said hi to everyone else and waved. Of course, there were rumors, but those were easy enough to steer clear of.

Several more laps in, she slowed her pace so she could cool down on the last lap and walk the last mile. It was a ritual for her to turn off her music so she could hear the sounds of nature— God's creations. This part of her run touched her heart. She always felt so close to her Savior.

Tucker was out on his front porch and waved as Kassidy made her last lap. She waved back and the hair stood up on the back of her neck. Something chilled her about the way he waved and smiled. A shudder ran down her spine. The uneasiness urged her to finish the walk to her house at a faster pace. The key didn't cooperate with the lock. Hands trembled as she tried to force it. The harder she tried, the worse she trembled.

At last, with the door closed behind her, she fumbled with the deadbolt. Her fingers failed to turn the switch to engage the lock but she finally grasped it in one final attempt. Maybe the officer was right when he suggested a dog would deter someone from breaking in. She'd go down to the animal shelter and look at the dogs they had.

Kassidy locked her bedroom door behind her. With heavy steps, she walked into her bathroom and locked that door too. Yet another first since she'd moved into her house.

Steam rolled over the top of the shower doors and with nervous energy from her run she quickly showered. While she dressed, it felt as if peering eyes could see. Her fingers meticulously wove her hair into a loose braid that fell halfway down her back. With a skip of her heart, she almost walked into her bedroom door when it didn't open. The lock that she hardly used, held the door securely in place, and she scolded herself for not unlocking it first. She was able to escape her bedroom, once she actually unlocked the door!

Light cascaded through the house as she opened every set of blinds and curtains in hopes to dispel the darkness that seemed to want to overwhelm her. She couldn't help but double check the locks as she passed from one room to the next.

Unease filled her and she half expected a hand to reach out and grab her from the shadows. She needed to run errands but was hesitant to leave, not knowing what she may find when she got home. Maybe her first errand would be to get better locks or another way to secure her house.

She'd seen alarms you could attach to windows and doors that emit a loud sound when opened. That sounded better than a dog she wasn't ready for.

She felt better with a plan in mind and grabbed the keys off the hook by the door. The drive to the local hardware store lacked any excitement, since there wasn't a single car on the road. Small city living didn't warrant much of a demand for alarms, so the store's selection wasn't great. Silently she counted the windows and doors in her house. She selected the appropriate number and walked to the register where a very cheerful employee waited to help her.

With her purchase in hand, she strolled out to her car. The heavy trunk lid popped up as she hit the button on the remote control. Her hand quickly covered her mouth as a gasp escaped. In the vast empty space of her trunk, there was a single red rose placed neatly in the center.

Two

SHE STAGGERED TWO STEPS back, unable to tear her eyes away from the rose. Droplets of glistening water still clung to the petals of the delicate flower.

She pulled her phone out of her pocket and dialed the police department for New Kingdom. They told her they would dispatch an officer to her.

Frantically, her eyes darted everywhere. She wasn't even sure what she looked for or whom. Would anyone look guilty? Her eyes swept the parking lot. Very few people were out and about this early. That was when she heard a car engine behind her in the parking lot. Fear gripped her as she spun on her heels, but relief washed over her face when she saw it was an officer.

A couple of car lengths away he put the cruiser in park then stepped out. With an air of authority about him, she wasn't sure she liked, he marched over. He wore mirrored sunglasses, and walked with that officer stride they were no doubt taught in the academy.

When he was a couple of feet from her, his towering form stopped and he gazed down at her. "What's the problem, ma'am?"

Already on the defensive, she said. "My name is Kassidy Parker, officer."

"Miss Parker, how can I help you today?" He looked at her with no emotion on his chiseled face.

"Um, that." Kassidy pointed to the pristine rose that lay in the open trunk.

He took a single step closer to peer into the trunk, as his hand rested on his holstered gun. He raised an eyebrow as he straightened up, "A rose, Miss Parker?"

"Yes, someone broke into my car and left that rose in the trunk."

"Are you sure it happened this morning?"

"Yes, I'm sure. Look at it. It's fresh and still has drops of water on it." Heat rushed to her face as the frustration began to build. An unmarked police car pulled in then parked next to the officer's car.

The man that exited from that car took her breath away. A polished badge clipped on one side of his hip, and a menacing gun on the other seemed to balance him out. He took his sunglasses off as he strolled over. His piercing blue eyes made her heart race as he made eye contact. She felt as if he studied her.

"Huffman, what do you have?" He asked as he leaned his upper body toward the trunk and glanced in.

"Detective Riggs, Miss Parker says someone broke into her car and left a rose." His voice belied any hint of concern as if he wasn't sure what to make of this. His muscles flexed in his face as he clenched his jaw, as if to ask, why call the police for such a trivial issue.

Detective Riggs returned to his normal towering height. "And you locked your car? Maybe a boyfriend wanted to leave this for you."

Kassidy stood her ground. "First of all, yes, I always lock my car. Secondly, I don't have a boyfriend. Thirdly I'm not sure if you are aware or not, but someone broke into my house yesterday."

"Could this have been left when they broke into your house?"

"No, I usually use my car when I leave the house so it wasn't in the garage when they broke in. This is fresh. There's no way this was in the trunk overnight or it would have wilted. Unless you know of a flower that doesn't wilt after being without water for hours?" She met his eyes; a scream lurked under the surface as she slowly exhaled.

"Huffman pull another report since this appears to be a separate incident." With strong well-manicured hands, he offered Kassidy his card, which said Detective Sawyer Riggs. "I'll be the detective handling your case. If you have any further information or questions, please call me."

"Thank you." Kassidy took his card while Officer Huffman placed the rose into a plastic bag.

A FEW DETERMINED STRIDES took Sawyer back to his car. Quick notes scribbled in his shorthand on his notepad would make it easy to finish the report. He watched Kassidy through his mirrored sunglasses. The way she carried herself made him almost believe that she told the truth. Granted nowadays, people called the police for things they did to themselves to get attention. Now, a rose in the trunk of a car wasn't the scariest thing he'd seen. Maybe it was just a secret admirer. If not, then this could quickly go wrong.

Finished with his notes, Sawyer glanced up to see Kassidy drop the bag in the trunk then slam the lid down. She hesitated at the driver's side door. He wasn't sure she would get in her car, but then she squared her shoulders and climbed behind the wheel. He could see her struggle and knew what had happened bothered her. The urge to keep her safe and catch whoever did this overwhelmed him. He felt a pull to her, but couldn't explain why.

He resisted the urge to follow her as he pulled out of the parking lot, hands clenched on the steering wheel, knuckles white. Maybe someone was following her. Unfortunately, besides dinner dishes and a rose, he had nothing to go on.

KASSIDY ENTERED THE grocery store and grabbed everything on her list in record time. Her heart raced as items passed across the scanner and her patience ran thin. This time no one would, she hoped, have time to get in her car. Home on her mind, she pictured the solid wood doors locked, and the accordion blinds closed to cast very little light around the sides. Panic rose up from her chest as the cashier took her time scanning each item. The slick plastic bags seemed to know her urgency to get home and played havoc with her fingers as she tried to grab the handles that seemed to have a mind of their own.

Sunglasses blocked the bright glare of the sun as she slid them down over her eyes. She rushed to her car. With her breath held, she opened the trunk.

Nothing.

Hot air rushed out of her lungs as she exhaled. After she placed the groceries in the trunk, she pushed the cart into the car corral. The corner of the metal cart met the metal corral and echoed through the parking lot, piercing the quiet morning. She cringed as the noise reached an annoying level. The tension in her shoulders told her it was time to go home.

To keep her imagination from running wild she turned up the music. That didn't work. She saw scrutinizing eyes in everyone she passed. Instead, she said a prayer to help ease her paranoia.

The interior garage door creaked as she slowly opened it. Why had she never noticed that before? There was no sound coming from her house. The mudroom seemed to stretch before her as if it had doubled in length for her to walk to the kitchen.

With her meager purchases in hand, the weight from the bags seemed to drag her shoulders down. After she put the groceries away, she set to work opening the ridiculously people-proof-plastic that encased her door and window alarms. The plastic became sharper than a knife after she cut it with scissors, ready to reach out and slice through delicate skin if she picked it up wrong.

As she freed the alarms from their plastic confinement, she laid them out, side by side. With the plastic packaging safely in the trash can, she opened the directions. She flipped the page over and over and stared intently at the grainy ink print. It felt as if she had missed something. Were the instructions this easy?

The hard-plastic alarm was small and wanted to slip out of her hands as she pulled the tab out of the battery compartment. The protective layer to the self-adhesive backing was elusive when she tried to peel it off. She couldn't get the corner of it to lift off with her fingernail. After several failed attempts, she saw a tab on the bottom she could easily grasp and lift off. Aligning the alarm with the edge of the back door she pressed it firmly onto the door. Next, she peeled the backing off the sensor and placed that on the doorframe and made sure the red dots were lined up to each other as per the instructions. With that done, she switched on the alarm then opened the back door. The horrendous shrieking noise the alarm made was enough to make her want to pull her hair out.

The alarm stopped when she slammed the door shut. Success. A smile crept up at the corners of her mouth. With a handful of alarms, she made short work of the rest of the doors. Now for the windows. After that task was completed, she stood back and surveyed her handy work. With a nod of her head, she felt satisfied that she had covered every entry point to her house.

Relief washed over her as her home became her safe haven again. Her shoulders dropped as her neck and shoulder muscles relaxed. She meandered down the hall to the kitchen with thoughts of lunch out on the deck on her mind. With a fresh crisp salad in hand, vinaigrette dressing in her other hand, she carefully balanced her drink and shuffled out to the deck to enjoy her lunch.

The weather was perfect. The breeze tousled through the wisps of hair that had come loose from her braid. The heat from the sun warmed her skin. She fought to open the umbrella to shade her while she ate as the wind made the fabric ripple, causing the umbrella to sway until it locked securely in place. Dark, eerie clouds brewed a storm on the horizon. A shadowy lining to the clouds told her she shouldn't take too long to eat—intense storms could be a force of nature you didn't want to be out in. The way the clouds were building, this could be one of those storms. At least she had her errands finished and didn't have plans for the rest of the day.

After lunch, she retreated inside. Quick steps led her back outside as she fought with the wind to take down the umbrella. The wind from a storm wouldn't hesitate to displace her umbrella and break it or whatever it landed on. Goosebumps greeted her as the temperature dropped several degrees from the wind. The sun seemed to hide from the imminent storm

Kassidy started to step away from the locked door when she remembered the alarm. She flipped the switch to on and double-checked the lock. All locked in.

As her house felt safe again, she made herself a cup of hot tea and headed to her favorite overstuffed chair that sat next to her front window. A good storm made for perfect reading weather. Teacup balanced perfectly on the saucer, she treaded lightly back into the living room, wary of sloshing the tea that threatened to escape over the delicate rim of the cup. After setting the cup and saucer down on the table next to the chair, she sank down into the plush fabric and picked up her book, opening it to where she'd left off. The jagged pages of her dad's old book were coarse against her soft hands.

Several minutes later, a clap of thunder announced the storm's arrival, startling Kassidy back to reality. Completely drawn into her book and the characters that lived there, she had missed the storm roll in. The trees violently swayed on the horizon as darkness loomed over her house. Enormous raindrops splattered on her porous concrete sidewalk. Soon, not a dry place was untouched by the onslaught of rain.

With a new cup of tea in her hands, she settled in to watch the storm. Her front yard looked out across a farm. The winds from the storm bent the cornstalks this way and that as if they danced in perfect harmony. The sky seemed to go on forever.

As she watched the storm, her mind seemed to ease about the recent events of the last two days. Everything would be fine; she snuggled back into the chair, sat her cup down, and drifted off to sleep with the accompaniment of the storm sounding in the background. The thunderous rumbles with the flashes of brilliant lightning were her lullaby.

Three

AN ALARM SHRIEKED SOMEWHERE in the house. She bolted up out of the chair as her quilt slid off her legs. Adrenaline shook the sleep from her mind. With eyes wide open, she looked around frantically to get her bearings.

Not able to hear anything over the obscenely loud alarm she marched from the living room toward the kitchen. Her heart raced as she neared the doorway. She pulled in a full breath; then slowly released it as she counted to ten. Kassidy hid behind the narrow wall, building up the nerve to peek around the doorframe. She closed her eyes and told herself to do it. She peeked fast and ducked back out of sight.

She saw no one. Just in that split second, a huge streak of lightning flashed across the sky, arced down and hit a tree in the distance while the explosion that was almost simultaneous rattled the windows. Kassidy screamed so loud it scared even her when it escaped.

She looked up toward the Heavens and stated, "That wasn't funny." Nervous laughter escaped as she stepped fully into the kitchen. A quick scan of her surroundings told her no one was there, but the back door was slightly open. The latch partially touching the metal plate on the doorframe made her heart rate accelerate. She knew she had locked the door before she went into the living room. Her hands trembled; then her whole body. There was no stopping the fear that now took hold of her. She distinctly knew she had locked the door because she had turned on the alarm first. She put her back to the door then reached behind her to close it.

The alarm immediately silenced, almost deafeningly so. Kassidy didn't move. She stood there and listened trying to hear any noise that didn't belong. Her hair stood up on the back of her neck. Unfortunately, all she heard was the roar of her own heartbeat in her ears.

Nothing seemed out of place or missing. Her eyes frantically swept the kitchen. One step at a time she reached her purse and with trembling fingers, snatched up her cell phone. After she dialed 911 with her thumb, she held it poised over the send button. She didn't want them to have to come out again today. With a baseball bat from the front closet hoisted over her shoulder, she just stood in the foyer and listened.

There was dead silence. Was he outside? Did he come into her house? She realized she didn't know which way to go. Should she chance staying in the house, or go outside? Was he waiting for her out there? Quick steps took her to the wall next to the couch in the foyer. She hid behind it. Her only possible option was to wait.

It was agonizing waiting behind a wall with a bat as her only defense. She waited until her phone's screensaver went off, telling her it had been five minutes. Maybe he hadn't been in her house. Wouldn't he have come out by now? She slid her phone into the back pocket of her jeans and said a silent prayer that he wasn't inside with her. Maybe the alarm had stopped him from entering.

The alarm screeched again. She fought to get her phone back out of her pocket. This time she didn't hesitate when she typed in 911 on the phone and hit the send button.

"New Kingdom 911. What's the address of your emergency?" The woman's voice on the other line calmly asked.

"7 RR M box 1008." Kassidy shook.

"What's the nature of your emergency?"

"I think someone was just in my house again!"

"Okay, we have officers on their way out to you. What makes you think that?"

"I bought alarms for my windows and doors today. The alarm sounded a few minutes ago, and the back door was open when I know I closed and locked it after lunch."

"And you're sure the storm didn't blow the door open? I mean, it's bad out there."

"Yes, because I closed it again when the alarm went off. It's open again; as I'm sure you can hear."

Her blood started to boil. What was wrong with people? How hard was it to believe what she said? Did anyone at the police department care about any of this?

"Yes, I hear the alarm. It's loud. I'm just asking if it's a possibility that the storm blew the door open." The dispatcher's condescending tone oozed through the phone.

"I'm sure no storm opened that door unless storms can magically unlock a deadbolt, or has something changed in that, that I need to know of?" Kassidy's tone matched that of the dispatcher's. She immediately scolded herself for letting the woman get to her.

"Ma'am, no, storms can't open deadbolts. But if you didn't have your door latched, a strong wind can blow them open."

"It was closed and locked."

"Okay, where are you in the house ma'am?"

"I'm hiding behind a wall in my front room."

"Can you see the back door from where you're at?"

"No, I don't want to come out from behind the wall."

"But you thought it was okay to stay in the house this whole time?" The dispatcher's tone belied any hint she knew the gravity of the situation.

"Just send the police. You're apparently not capable of understanding what's going on. The officers can come in the back door; you know the one with the loud alarm." With that, Kassidy hung up on the rude dispatcher and shoved her phone in her pocket.

Time seemed to slow down to a crawl, the second hand on the clock in her living room announced every second that passed. It felt as if every muscle in her body needed to move and that if they didn't, they would seize from being in the same spot for too long.

"Police!" boomed a voice from the kitchen

"I'm in the living room." Kassidy's voice cracked.

"Stay there we'll come to you."

Her grip instinctively tightened on the bat at the sight of two officers and Detective Riggs as they rounded the wall.

"Ma'am, can you please put that bat down?" One officer held up his hand toward her.

"Oh, yeah sorry." Kassidy propped the bat against the wall.

"Miss Parker, are you okay?" Sawyer motioned for her to follow him to the kitchen while the other two officers continued to clear the house.

She watched them disappear down the dark hallway with guns drawn then turned to follow Detective Riggs.

"Miss Parker?" Sawyer's eyes pierced right through her.

"I'm sorry, what?" Kassidy stammered. She rose up on tiptoes to switch the alarm off.

"Are you okay?" Sawyer asked. Kassidy flinched as he gently touched her shoulder.

"Yes, I'm fine. What about the basement and garage?"

"They'll check those while we talk." Sawyer motioned with his arm to the stool at the kitchen counter.

Kassidy turned to him as she perched on it and tried to ask in a steady voice, "How's someone getting in my house?"

"Does anyone have a key beside you?" Sawyer reached for his ever-faithful small spiral notebook and pen.

"No. No one has ever had a key as long as I've lived here." Kassidy hoped this wouldn't be a repeat of previous calls where she felt no one believed her.

"An ex-boyfriend maybe, that wants you back?"

"No." Heat rushed into her cheeks. "I haven't dated or had anyone in my life for a while."

"Have you ever gone out of town and given someone a key to check on things?"

"No, I don't travel."

"Ever lose a set of keys or misplace them?"

"No, never. I'm someone who knows where everything is in my house."

The officers came back into the kitchen. "Did you find anything, officers?" Sawyer turned to face them.

One officer tried to discreetly roll his eyes at Sawyer but Kassidy saw. "Nothing, sir. No signs of forced entry at all. Figure someone got a hold of a set of keys."

"No one has a set of keys!" She gestured to the key rack which showed shiny keys on every hook available. "Look!"

"Miss Parker, calm down. We have to look at all the possibilities."

"Why don't you look at the possibility that someone's breaking into my house and I don't know why or how."

"Miss Parker, please tell us what happened today since the incident with the rose in the trunk at the hardware store." Sawyer gave a slight head nod to the officer who also took out his notepad.

Kassidy's voice turned monotone as she walked them through the events that lead them to where they were now.

Sawyer finished his notes and turned toward the door. "Can you lock it as you did earlier before the alarm sounded, please?"

This door was one of her favorite parts of the house and the fact it was a beautiful French door didn't hurt. She lifted the nickel-plated lever handle. They heard three bolts slide into place. With trembling fingers that fumbled with the lock, she finally flipped the latch then faced the officers again. "That's all you need to do, and it's more than securely locked. There are three bolts on this door that secure it in place so there's no way the wind from any storm, short of a tornado, can open that door."

The officer who had been so skeptical couldn't meet her stare. Sawyer reached forward and pushed down on the lever doorknob. Nothing happened. "So even from the inside, you can't just push on the doorknob to unlock and open this door?"

"No, you have to unlock it again then push down on the lever." Why so many questions about her lock? Shouldn't they concern themselves with how someone came through the locked door? She was patient because she needed them to believe her.

"I agree with you. No way a storm blew this door open. Did you put these on?" Sawyer pointed to the unimpressive alarm.

"Yes, on every door and window when I got home from the hardware store. That's why I went there today—to buy them." Kassidy couldn't tell if he was mocking her or not.

"They're not a bad idea. Some alarm systems are expensive. So if you can't afford one, these usually deter someone from coming in when they go off." Sawyer smiled at her.

"Thanks."

"Okay, I think that's all. Will you be alright?" The concern in his voice made her glance up and meet his eyes. She hoped it was genuine concern and not just a standard question he asked before he left a person's house.

"I'll be fine. What do I do now?"

"We'll add this to what we already have. Do you know of anyone who would want to do this? Someone with the wrong idea?" Sawyer's smoldering eyes cut right through her and made her pulse race.

No one came to mind; especially no one who would break into her house. "No, I really don't."

"Well, if you think of anyone or anything, call us." He turned on his heel then disappeared out the door as the officers trailed after him.

With the door locked yet again, she reached up and switched the alarm back on. She turned around and just stared at her house. The fact that someone had been in her house while she dozed in her chair did nothing to calm her uneasy nerves.

Stiff legged, she marched into the living room, picked up her teacup, and took it back to the kitchen to wash along with the rest of the dishes in the sink. Her stomach told her she needed to eat something. She hadn't eaten much yesterday, so she didn't feel bad about how much pork fried rice she piled on her plate now! Hunger was a great motivator to overeat. With her stomach satiated, she busied herself with washing and putting away the dishes. They clinked as she placed the clean ones on top of the stacks already in her cabinets. Even with her hands busy, her mind wandered to today's events.

Maybe music would drown out those thoughts, at least for a little while. She turned up her favorite Christian radio station and sang along. Her mind kept replaying the officer's questions about if someone had a key. She'd never changed her locks when she moved into the house years earlier. To be honest, she'd never thought about it. The previous owner had laid several keys on the counter for her when they'd moved out. If someone did have a copy of the key, then the only common-sense thing to do was change the locks.

Locksmiths were few and far between in the town she lived in. The second one she spoke with, she liked right away and scheduled them to change the locks the next day. They agreed with the short timeframe requested due to the circumstances.

Nausea hit her stomach, causing her hand to fly to her mouth. Several seconds passed before she realized her food wasn't going to make a reappearance. She hoped that with the locksmith scheduled it would help relieve some of her stress and make her house a fortress no one could get into. She crossed back to the kitchen and turned off the radio on her way. Maybe some nighttime tea would help her sleep and hopefully calm her stomach. With teacup in hand, she retired to her bedroom after a quick trip around to check all the doors and windows. The lock on the bedroom door was not intimidating enough to keep someone out. She shoved the chair that was never used - except for the purpose of collecting dust she had to clean - under the doorknob. That seemed to help ease her tension for a bit.

Maybe TV or a movie would help take her mind off things. Startled when her phone rang, she spilled the tea on her bed. She raced into the bathroom for a hand towel as she answered her phone. "Hello."

Nothing.

"Hello."

Faint breaths came through the phone. She yanked the phone from her ear. Caller ID said "unavailable". She scolded herself for answering an unavailable number. She hung up and blocked that call when her phone rang again. She almost dropped it and juggled it to keep it from landing on the floor. It was her best friend, Celeste.

"Hey, Celeste." Kassidy continued to clean up her spilled tea that was now just a faint brown smear on her taupe sheets.

"Hey, are we still on for lunch tomorrow?"

"Oh shoot, I have a locksmith coming over to change all the locks on my house." She never forgot appointments or lunch dates with friends. This was another part of her life this lunatic was affecting.

"Wow, that's not like you. Kass, what's going on?"

Kassidy spilled everything to Celeste. Celeste had been one of her best friends from childhood and Henry, her husband, was also a very dear friend. Kassidy couldn't have been happier when they'd got married. It wasn't a perfect marriage, but there's no such thing. They both loved Jesus Christ and only grew stronger in their marriage with their trials and tribulations.

Kassidy hoped to find that one day, but she was also happy with where her life was now. True, she didn't have to work due to the inheritance left to her by her parents and aunt. But she didn't spend more than she needed to and that meant she could live without worries of money issues for the rest of her life. She wasn't rich by any means but she was comfortable and able to take comfort that she would never have that stress.

"Henry and I can come spend the night, or you come over here?" Worry and concern flooded through the phone from her friend.

"A locksmith's coming over tomorrow, so I should be fine tonight. I have all the windows and doors locked. I even have my bedroom door locked and a chair wedged under the door handle." Kassidy giggled at that last part, which caused Celeste to laugh.

"Well call if you change your mind, or if you need anything. You know Henry and I love you and would do anything for you." Celeste's voice caught in her throat.

"I feel the same. I'll call if I need anything but I also won't hesitate to call the police."

"Okay, goodnight Kass. Talk to you tomorrow after the locksmith comes out."

"Night, Celeste." Kassidy hung up and felt better knowing someone believed her. It wouldn't have surprised her if they showed up on her doorstep. She'd never had better friends than Celeste and Henry—they'd always check on her.

An upbeat, feel-good movie played on the movie channel so she sunk down into her pile of pillows and almost disappeared. Not even halfway through the movie, her eyelids drooped as she started to doze off. A quick press of the remote threw her bedroom into total darkness. Halfway rolled over, she was asleep before she knew it.

Four

KASSIDY REACHED HER arms above her head and pointed her toes toward the end of the bed. She held that position for several moments while all her muscles stretched. She couldn't even remember waking at all while she slept. As she rolled over to face the door, she had to stifle a scream. The chair no longer secured the door but instead, ominously faced the bed. Only inches away from where she lay, indentions in her comforter told her someone had rested their feet on the edge of the bed as if they had sat there and watched her sleep.

Slowly, she slipped from the bed and dropped to the floor, so she didn't disturb the foot impressions, then felt around on the top of the nightstand for the phone. Detective Riggs' direct line rang several times before he answered. "Detective Riggs."

"Detective, this is Kassidy Parker. I'm not sure if you remember me or not from yesterday, but I think you need to get back to my house. Someone watched me sleep last night."

"I'll be right there with another officer. Don't touch anything."

Kassidy chaotically threw on clothes. A few steps toward the door, she hesitated. She knew nothing would happen to her if she walked between the chair and bed, but her legs didn't want to cooperate with her mind's common sense. Inch by inch she quietly passed between them, and then sprinted down the hall to the back door.

Nothing else seemed out of the ordinary as she made it to the back door and she was happy to see officers and Detective Riggs pull into her driveway. She unlocked the door.

"Miss Parker?"

"Let me show you." Kassidy slowly walked down the hallway toward her room. The officers towered over her as they trailed behind her.

They reach the door to her room, where she swept her arm toward the chair. The officer who had been at the hardware store and her house yesterday stared at her in disbelief. His jaw tightened as he clamped his mouth shut. His lips became a thin white line.

"Yes ma'am, it's a chair. Anything special we need to know about it?"

Kassidy put her hands on her hips. "Yes, there is. First, you can drop the attitude as if I'm wasting your time. Second, I placed that up under the door handle last night before I went to sleep. When I got up this morning, someone had moved it to where it is now. And if you notice the bed, there are imprints as if someone propped their feet up and watched me sleep."

"Officer, stow the attitude and take pictures of this. Miss Parker, when did you go to sleep and what time did you wake up?" Detective Riggs studied the chair and the bed.

Kassidy couldn't believe the nerve of these officers. She'd never had to call the police before, so she wasn't sure if this was their normal attitude toward citizens. But she didn't like it one bit. They almost treated her as if she'd done this herself.

The officer moseyed out to his car and retrieved his camera. Kassidy noticed there was no sense of urgency at all. The shutter clicked on the camera as he photographed the bed and chair, while Kassidy told Detective Riggs and the other officer everything.

"Miss Parker, may I suggest changing your locks? Apparently, someone you don't know has gotten a key at some point and has access to your home."

"Detective, I've already called to have a locksmith come out today."

"Miss Parker, do you drink?"

"Excuse me?" Kassidy glared at the officer and took a step forward. "What are you saying? That I'm a drunk that does things I don't remember?"

"No, I'm just asking to get all the facts and put all the evidence together." He faltered.

"No, I don't drink. I had an alcoholic uncle who abused then killed, my aunt. He's serving a life sentence. I even lost my parents over it. She was my mom's only living relative and my dad was an only child. They died in a car crash racing to the hospital the last time he put my aunt in the emergency room. I made a promise to myself I would never touch a drop of alcohol. By the way, she died the next day."

"Sorry...I didn't mean..." The officer stammered and looked at Detective Sawyer with wide eyes.

"Take that to the station and log it into evidence, officers. Thank you." Sawyer didn't look at Kassidy but stepped between her and the officer. The stern look he gave the officer was hard to miss.

As the officers walked out of the bedroom, she could feel the tension and heard the one mutter to the other. "I still say she did this."

"Excuse me?" Kassidy's nails dug into her palms as she clenched her fist. Her anger was fueled by the unthoughtful officer's insensitive comment.

By the look on his face and his wide eyes when he turned around, the officer hadn't intended for her to hear him. Detective Riggs held up his hand in front of her as if he might need to hold her back.

"Let me show you something. Are you done with pictures?" Kassidy asked, matter-of-factly.

"Yes, ma'am." The officer wouldn't look at her.

"So, I can sit in the chair and show you something?" Kassidy stared at the officer who had made the comment, waiting for him to answer.

"Yes, ma'am." The tiny head tilt to his partner caught Kassidy's eye.

"There are no marks in the carpet from the chair, except by the door and where the chair's at now, right?"

"No, ma'am."

Kassidy plopped down in the chair and heaved her legs up as if to rest them on the edge of the bed, only they hit air and fell to the floor. Her legs were not long enough to extend to the bed unless she practically lay down in the chair.

"Did you catch that, officer?"

"Yes, ma'am."

"Now look at the size of my feet; they are a size six. Do the indentions look like they are that small to you?" Kassidy held up one of her feet several inches off the floor, so he could see the size difference, and then swept her arm toward the bed where the indentions were much larger than her tiny feet.

"I'm sorry about that, Miss Parker. He meant nothing by that. It's just part of the investigation; it's not personal. We're just covering our bases." Sawyer met her eyes with a powerful gaze.

"I don't appreciate the cynicism from the officers when I call asking for help. And the drinking comment is a sore subject with me. I'm sorry." Kassidy knew she should apologize to the officer, but she couldn't. She needed to calm down before she even attempted to.

"That's okay." Sawyer turned to the officers. "That's all. Go log that into evidence and we'll talk when I get back to the station. What time's the locksmith coming over?" He asked as he turned back toward her.

"What? Oh, um, three forty-five."

"We can have an officer here until they arrive."

"I'll call friends and have them come over and stay until the locks are changed."

"Okay. I'll stay until they get here. With what happened, I think this will only get worse before we can catch who's doing this. I'd say someone's taken an interest in you, Miss Parker. I'll have the officers step up patrols in the area. Maybe we can catch the culprit coming or going. I don't mean to alarm you, but this could get ugly."

"Thank you." She was grateful she wouldn't be alone. "How bad do you think it could get?"

"Well, some of these cases have horrible outcomes. It's hard to prove without eyewitness accounts or evidence to link to the person. And with how careful they've been so far, this could get messy."

"Well, changing the locks today means they won't be able to get back in. I never changed the locks when I moved in so who knows who may have had a key to this place."

"I'm glad you could get an appointment today. Hopefully, you're right and it'll deter, whoever's watching you. Maybe they'll leave you alone."

"Thanks, I hope so too. I feel like I can't even do my normal activities."

"Like what? You know you should always change your routine so it's not repetitive."

"Well, I run every morning, have my weekly Bible study, and go to church on Sundays. Morning and evening services. Different things like that."

"What if you changed when you run? Say, in the afternoon instead of the morning or change your route?"

"I can definitely change my route. I'll map out how far a mile is and just do a different loop. Or I could go to a park and run on the trails?"

"Yes, that'll help. Call your friends and I'll stick around until they get here."

Kassidy walked around the bed to get her phone from the nightstand but when she looked at the chair, she couldn't bring herself to walk past it again.

Detective Riggs saw her hesitation, grabbed the chair, and then raised it a couple of inches further to ask where it needed to go. She pointed to the corner, so he would be able to see the indentions in the carpet where the chair normally sat. He strolled back over, swept his hand over the comforter and made the footmarks disappear as if they'd never been there.

With the chair moved, Kassidy found she was able to walk around to her side of the bed. She grabbed her cell phone to call Celeste. Her conversation was short, and her friends didn't hesitate to jump in the car and head over to her house.

"They'll be here shortly. You can go. They live less than five minutes away."

"No, I'm sorry, detective's orders!" He smiled at her as heat flooded her cheeks.

They walked down the hallway toward the kitchen and Kassidy smiled to see Celeste and Henry walk in the back door and gave her a big hug.

"Celeste and Henry, this is Detective Riggs. He's handling my case."

They shook hands all around and then an awkward silence filled the room.

Detective Riggs fiddled with his pen and notebook. "Well, if you guys can stay with her until all the locks are changed, I'd appreciate that."

"Yes sir, we have no plans so we can be here all day," Henry assured Detective Riggs.

"Thanks. Miss Parker, I'll get to the station and get all of this added to the reports we already have open, and see what we can find."

With that, Sawyer turned to leave then turned back toward the kitchen and looked around once more before he darted out the door. Kassidy closed and locked the back door.

Five

"OH, MY GOSH! KASS, what's going on?" Celeste filled the kettle for tea.

Kassidy filled them in on the night's events and Henry let out a low whistle.

"Kass we need to make sure this house is more secure. How did he get in here and turn off the alarm, unlock doors and move a chair from behind another locked door without you hearing?" Henry's eyes squinted as he inspected the back door.

"I have a locksmith coming over so that'll take care of the locks. I have no clue what's going on or who it could be." Kassidy sank down onto a stool at the counter and shook her head, tossing a lock of hair over her shoulder.

"Well the new locks will keep him out; then the police can do their job and arrest him." Celeste, always the optimist in the group!

"Well, I need a shower so I'll be back. Hold down the fort for me, would you?" Kassidy smiled and trotted down the hall with a bounce in her step for the first time in a couple of days.

She took longer than usual in the shower since she knew nothing would happen with her friends down the hall in the kitchen. Steam covered the mirrors. She threw jeans and a hoodie on then met her friends in the kitchen. It was only nine forty-five in the morning and they still had six hours to kill before the locksmith would get there.

"So how do you want to spend the next six hours?" Kassidy was glad her friends were here but she didn't want to force them to stay in the house if they didn't want to.

"Well, we could check out the antique mall. What do you think?" A mischievous smile played at the corners of Celeste's dainty mouth.

Henry threw his two cents in. "Well, I for one don't want to leave the house to whoever's been breaking in. I'd rather stay here since we know he isn't in here now, get the locks changed and then leave later if we want to go somewhere. I'd rather not chance him getting in again."

"I agree with Henry. I would feel better being here and then we can go out after they change the locks. Sorry, Celeste."

"Hey, no skin off my back. What do you feel like doing? We could continue our slaughter of Henry at cards." Celeste playfully elbowed Henry as Kassidy chuckled.

"No! We can play any other game but you two cheat when you play cards." Henry pointed back and forth between the two and passed a guilty judgment.

Kassidy folded her lean arms over her chest. "We don't cheat. We just might know each other well enough that we know what the other is thinking."

"Well, that's cheating in my book because I can never win against you two." Henry pushed his bottom lip out.

"Okay, how about board games? Or we could continue our old black and white movie marathon?"

"Either one of those sounds good, but I suggest breakfast first. I could make my famous blueberry pancakes?" Henry held up the insulated bag he had brought with him.

"Now you see why I keep him around don't you?" Celeste hopped off the stool to grab plates and silverware.

"I'll grab the movies." Kassidy practically skipped down the hall.

Settled in with their breakfast and the marathon of movies set up, they said a prayer to let the changing of the locks deter the person stalking Kassidy and let them give up their pursuit of scaring and tormenting her. A couple of movies in, they took a break to make a snack-lunch of fruit, vegetables, and granola with smoothies.

"Thanks guys, I feel much better. I needed this today." Kassidy couldn't express how grateful she was. She wasn't anxious or scared in her house when she had her friends with her. She felt at ease and didn't expect any dark lurking shadow to actually be a person.

"Hey, no problem. I wish you would have told us you were dealing with this." Henry put a hand on her shoulder.

Kassidy grabbed a plate and moved into the living room. "I didn't want to bother you guys. I can't believe this is happening."

"Well, I'm glad you did. We called the church and put it on the prayer chain. Hopefully, with enough people praying for the police to catch this person, it'll happen." Celeste and Henry joined Kassidy in the living room and they settled in for another movie.

About halfway through the next movie, Kassidy's phone rang. It showed "unavailable" so she swiped her thumb across the reject button and continued to watch the movie, thinking nothing of it.

After the end of the first movie, they took a break to get ready for the locksmith. Kassidy and Celeste washed then put away all the dishes, while Henry ran down to the store to grab a few groceries for dinner. They discussed dinner in, grilling on the deck and watching the sunset while they ate.

Today was a great day. Kassidy hardly thought about her stalker, if you could call him that. She didn't feel the tension pulling in her neck like she had the day before. Although, it was troublesome to know there was someone out there doing this with no clue why or even who it was. She reeled at the thought that she could have done something to start this. No one jumped out in her mind as someone who would be capable of such a thing.

A few minutes before three forty-five, the locksmith, Collin, showed up and did a walk through to inspect all the doors to her house. He suggested what locks he would use to keep the intruder from getting in again. He had pamphlets and comparison charts to show Kassidy all the features and capabilities of the locks. After they had looked at several, Collin suggested a few that were more expensive, but were pretty much pick proof and couldn't be bumped into opening, like a few that Kassidy had seen on the news.

With her mind made up, Kassidy chose the more expensive ones; she loved the beautiful intricacies and sturdiness of the locks. They added beauty to her door with their flat nickel finish she was so fond of. But most of all, they gave her the security and protection she longed to have again in her once impenetrable home.

An hour and a half later, the locksmith finished. Kassidy paid him and included a generous tip for the great work. His rough hands from years of manual labor stretched out and dropped the keys to her new pristine locks into her hands. He also installed block bars on the windows. They were hard to see from the outside and meant that no one could raise the windows when the bars were in place. If someone wanted to get in, they would make a lot of noise and that would alert anyone in the house.

"I'd also suggest a dog. No one really wants to deal with a large menacing dog when it's staring at you through the window. That has better luck in keeping people out than locks, usually." Collin nodded his head as he bounded down the steps to his battered work van.

"Thanks, I really appreciate everything you did today." Kassidy waved from the back door.

"That's not a bad idea, Kass. We could go to the shelter and see what they have." Celeste loved animals but Kassidy had never had a pet before. She was leery of what it would entail to keep a pet healthy and happy.

"Oh, I don't know Celeste; I'm not sure I want a pet." Kassidy pictured a dog as it chewed on her couch, stuffing protruded from its foamy saliva drenched mouth.

"Oh, come on, we can just look. It doesn't mean we have to get you one."

"Hun, don't push if she doesn't want a dog. It wouldn't be a good idea to force one on her. You have to be ready to have a pet—they take a lot of time and care, especially dogs." Henry backed up Kassidy and she sighed in relief.

"How about we look at dogs if these new locks don't work and the creep keeps getting in." Kassidy scanned her quaint undisturbed non-dog-chewed front room furniture.

"Yeah okay I'll keep an eye open for the right dog for you. And I get to be the one who takes you to get one if it comes down to that, okay?"

Kassidy chuckled, "Deal."

Kassidy fought with the old keyrings to put on the new ones. Metal scraped from the keys that she shoved onto the unforgiving cold steel rings that seemed to be in defiance of any change. Several minutes later she hung them up on the hooks back where they called home.

Henry looked up at the clock and suggested dinner.

"Sure, where at?" Kassidy felt that her house was a fortress again with the new stronghold of locks that barred any uninvited visitors.

"I thought you wanted to stay in and eat on the deck?" Henry asked.

"With the new locks, I feel like going out."

"I feel like Italian, if you want my opinion." Celeste bobbed her head side to side.

"You always want Italian." Henry nudged his wife then slipped his arm around her tiny waist.

"Yes, I do. But I could go for any place that serves pasta."

"How about Sammy's? They have just about everything there." Kassidy grabbed her new keys. The sharpness of the unused metal scrapped against her palm and caused her to loosen her grip on them.

"Sammy's sounds good. What about you, Hun?" Henry turned toward Celeste.

"Deal. We'll drive, Kass. We can bring you home and have Henry check out the house before we head home ourselves."

Kassidy grabbed her coat. With the way the temperatures dipped in the evenings, she had no doubt she would be shivering and teeth chattering when they drove her home after their meal.

She locked the door behind her and turned to see that Henry watched her.

"What, making sure I know the delicate intricacies of locking a door?"

"No," he laughed.

"Right, sure, go ahead and mock me but someone's been getting in my house. I know when I've locked a door and that someone has been getting through that locked door."

"I know, Kass. Don't be mad. We're just worried about you." Celeste started down the stairs to the car.

The drive to the restaurant was short even though Kassidy lived on the other side of town. Even knowing the menu inside and out, Kassidy couldn't decide what she was in the mood for—everything sounded mouth-watering. Celeste was first to decide on lasagna, with Henry going with his usual steak. The waiter walked over and Kassidy nodded to Celeste and Henry to order first. The waiter diligently wrote down each request on her trusty order book then stared at Kassidy. Kassidy decided on the grilled chicken in parmesan sauce over linguini; the thought of that first bite made her stomach rumble quietly. The waiter left with their orders and came back with breadsticks and water for everyone.

"Thanks again for today, guys. I needed the distraction. The thought of someone being in my house or watching me is so frightening." Kassidy shuddered.

"I can't imagine what you're going through. I'm so glad I have Henry. I'd be scared to death if I lived alone." Celeste grabbed Henry's hand on the table and squeezed.

"You know, there's a couple of great guys that go to church if you want me to introduce you." A mischievous smile played at the corners of Henry's mouth.

"Oh no, I'm fine. I'll find someone in my own time."

They made small talk over the next several minutes, when Kassidy noticed out of the corner of her eye that Detective Riggs had walked in. Celeste saw Kassidy divert her eyes and looked up as the Detective walked past their table.

"Hey, isn't that the detective who was at your house today?"

"Yes, he's the one working my case."

"Did you smile when you said that?" Henry pried.

"Stop it! Don't you two start something I'll have to clean up!"

Steam rolled off their food as the waitress set the plates down. Everything was cooked to perfection. Each of them inhaled over their plate, savoring the aromas that drifted up from their prepared meals. Juices from Henry's steak flowed freely through the empty paths around the potatoes and vegetables, while sauce clung to every piece of pasta heaped in the middle of Kassidy's plate.

They bowed their heads and said a quiet prayer for their food, asking for the wisdom of the officers and Detective to find the culprit and stop them.

Kassidy said, "Amen," and then raised her head to find Detective Riggs watching her.

He smiled. She gave a little wave then immediately dropped her eyes to her plate and took her first bite, savoring the flavors that mixed and blended as she swallowed the impeccable food.

"You know, he's not half bad looking, Kass. Is he single?" Celeste prodded.

"I don't know, Celeste. I won't date the person who's working on my case. And I have no clue if he's a born-again Christian or not." Kassidy refused to look up from her food.

"You know, I don't see a ring on his finger," Henry added.

Kassidy picked up a breadstick, armed and ready to toss it at either one of them. "Oh my gosh; stop it you two!"

"Okay, okay, just don't throw that at us. We may have to call him over for assault with a breadstick!" Henry held up his hands in surrender.

Kassidy set the breadstick down and her cheeks flushed red when she saw Detective Riggs still watching her, smiling as he held in a laugh.

Oh no, had he heard any of their conversation?

They finished their food with minimal conversation and then Kassidy asked for a to-go box. She loved that she always got two meals from the huge portions at Sammy's. Henry snagged the check within a second of the waitress placing it on the table.

"No guys, I should buy. You kept me company all day and drove to the restaurant."

"Nope, too late; they already took our money." Celeste smiled as she got up and headed toward the door and Henry and Kassidy followed.

Kassidy tried to sneak a peek at Detective Riggs, but was caught in the act as he waved goodbye a second before she was out the door.

At the car, she slid into the back seat with her to-go box next to her then fumbled to put her coat on. It was a quiet ride home. They were all full and content with their meal. She tilted her head back and watched the sky through the back windshield.

Henry turned to Celeste, as they pulled into the driveway. "Did you want to wait here or come in while I check the house?"

"I'll wait in the car." Celeste tilted her head toward Kassidy. "You don't mind, do you?"

"Of course not. I'll talk to you tomorrow." Kassidy hopped out of the car with keys in hand.

"Here, I'll go in first and check everything out." Henry held out his hand.

With the keys passed off, she waited at the bottom of the three small steps that led up to her deck at the back door, shifting from one foot to the next. Her heart thundered in her chest at the thought of someone being in the house waiting for her. Henry easily unlocked the door and disappeared inside. Kassidy checked her watch then glanced at Celeste as he came back out.

"Did you want to check everything out real quick to make sure everything's where you left it?" Henry stood to the side while Kassidy passed by him to get into the house.

First she scrutinized the kitchen. Satisfied, she dropped her purse with a thud onto the counter and set her food next to it. After a quick check of the rooms, she found no one lurking in a dark corner or in the closets. She gave a sigh of relief—finally she had her home back. Henry waited at the back door, propped against the counter.

With a nod she let him know everything was okay. He gave her a quick one-armed hug and bounded down the stairs to the car.

Glancing back, he said, "Lock up tonight and call us no matter what. I don't care what time it is."

"I promise." Kassidy waved and saw Celeste wave back from the front seat.

She double-checked the lock and turned on the alarm anyway. With her back to the door, she analyzed everything as if seeing it for the first time. Shadows were the dark hiding places of evil, which seemed to twist and contort until her imagination ran wild. She shook her head and closed her eyes. When she opened them again, the shadows no longer held the boogeyman ready to snatch her as she walked by.

With her food placed in the cool confines of the refrigerator, she proceeded to the front room to watch one more movie before bed: one of her favorite black and white movies, with big stars and an ending where the good guys always win. She tucked her feet under her then covered herself with her grandmother's quilt. She played with the delicate edges with her fingers, a habit she'd had since she was a little girl when her grandmother had made it for her.

Six

DRAWN INTO THE MOVIE she almost felt normal and safe in her house. She flipped sideways in the overstuffed chair; her legs and feet dangled over the arm. The phone rang and interrupted her thoughts. Startled by it ringing this late, she stared at her phone as it rang a second time. She was hesitant to pick it up and see who would call at this hour; almost sure it would be *him*. She sighed in relief. It read "Celeste" on the caller ID.

"Hello." Kassidy cheerfully answered.

"Kassidy?" A male's voice asked.

"Who's this?" Angry that her voice shook, she knew it wasn't Henry on the other line.

"Did you have fun at dinner?" The male asked.

"Who is this?" She sat up straight and covered her mouth with her hand.

"That's not nice to not answer a question when it is asked. Did. You. Have. Fun. At. Dinner?"

Kassidy hung up the phone as her hands started to sweat. When the phone rang again, she jumped, almost dropped it, but caught it in midair.

Unlike last time, "unavailable" showed on the caller ID. She answered anyway.

"Listen, I don't know who you are or what you want, but leave me alone," Kassidy spat before he could say anything.

"Miss Parker?" She jumped when she realized it was a different male's voice.

"Hello?" She bent forward and put her head in her free hand.

"This is Detective Riggs. Are you okay?" The concern was unmistakable.

"Did you call a couple of minutes ago?" Kassidy practically yelled the question as she jumped up out of the chair.

"This is the only time I've called your number, Miss Parker."

"So, you didn't just call asking if I had fun at dinner?"

"No, and if he asked that, then he's watching you. Did you see anyone that stood out to you at Sammy's?"

Kassidy wasn't sure how she felt about the Detective being at the restaurant and now on the phone. Had he called a few minutes ago and was now calling as a distraction so she wouldn't think he was the first caller?

"Why are you calling me, Detective?"

"Miss Parker, I'm going to come over and make sure there isn't anyone outside your house. Okay?" Kassidy heard a car engine start in the background through Sawyer's phone.

"No, you don't have to do that. I'm fine. I had the locks changed today, so no one has a key anymore."

"It's no trouble. I'm not far. I can be there in less than ten minutes." She heard him gun his engine. She ran to the doors and ran her hands over the locks to make sure they were all secure. What a perfect way for someone to control a situation of stalking if he worked at a police department. He could make any evidence seem inconsequential and even make it disappear with no one being the wiser. Was that why the other officers were so nonchalant with her when she called?

"Detective Riggs, I really think it would be a waste of your time. I really am okay."

Kassidy's voice was firm. Maybe he wouldn't feel the need to check on her. Unless he was the one who had been in her house and wanted an excuse to come see her again.

"Listen, Miss Parker, I can hear the fear in your voice. Something doesn't sound right. I'd feel better if I checked on things, just to make sure." Sawyer's voice was smooth and calm.

The voice in the back of her mind told her not to trust him. In fact, it screamed it. Her mom had always told her to trust her gut instinct. It hadn't steered her wrong before so she would trust it now. She sprinted to the closet and snatched up her Louisville Slugger. With her baseball bat in hand, she crept to the corner in the living room and crouched behind a chair.

She heard tires on gravel as headlights splashed across her kitchen, blinding anything in their path. She stifled a cry behind her fist and prayed to be strong. Knots cramped her stomach as the food she had eaten earlier threatened to reappear. Maybe if she showed a good front then whoever was doing this, even if it was Detective Riggs, would see it was a wasted effort. She wouldn't roll over and play dead for anyone.

Thunderous knocks at her back door made her jump. She repositioned herself in the crouched position behind the chair and heard her ankle pop. The kitchen windows shook as a result of the frantic pounding.

Slowly, she rose from her crouched position. She peered around the doorway in the living room to the back door. An enormous shadow filled the entire glass of the door. With a deep breath, she crossed to the doorway with slow determined steps. She turned on the light, as she hid behind the wall next to the door.

"Who is it?" Kassidy asked so quietly she wasn't sure they would hear her on the other side.

"Miss Parker, it's Detective Riggs."

"Did you see anyone outside?"

"No. Are you going to open the door?" The concern in his voice stirred something in her.

"I'm okay. I'm just going to go to bed. I told you not to waste a trip."

Sawyer saw her through the door now that she'd moved away from the wall. She still clung to the bat. "Miss Parker, if you're okay, why are you holding a bat?"

She glanced down. With the death grip with which she held the bat, her knuckles had turned ghastly white.

The phone rang. She jerked her head up and stared right into his eyes. He raised his hands. He didn't have a phone. She crossed to the living room. The caller ID showed that it was Celeste. Her hands shook as she dropped the bat on the hardwood floor. With a single step back, so she could see Detective Riggs, she answered the phone.

"Why is he at your house?" Hate filled the other end of the phone.

"Miss Parker, open the door!" Sawyer must have seen the fear in her eyes as a single tear rolled down her cheek.

As she took a step toward the door, there was movement out of the corner of her eye. He was in her house with her! Sawyer saw the movement and kicked frantically at the door.

With a step back, she closed the distance to the front door and had it unlocked as a hand snaked her waist. A scream erupted from her that was so loud it startled the person who had grabbed her. They let go.

The front door flew in as she yanked on the door handle, causing the alarm to shriek. She sprinted through the front yard into the farmer's field in front of her house. In a matter of seconds, she had raced down rows of cornstalks. The leaves and husks reached for her. Hands held up in front of her face took the brunt of the abuse. Detective Riggs yelled but she couldn't hear what he saying over the roar of her heartbeat in her ears.

Someone crashed through the corn behind her as she pumped her arms and legs, cutting a line through the crops. Panic wanted to take hold, and she'd never been so glad she'd run for years to condition her for this moment...Although, she hadn't run all those years in hopes for a moment like this!

Heavy footsteps caught up with her from behind. She darted to her left to lose the attacker when an arm wrapped around her waist and pulled her to him. The other one covered her mouth to muffle her scream. They both landed on rock hard soil, with enormous fissures, that hadn't seen rain in weeks.

Kassidy started to fight when she heard him whisper in her ear. "Shh, shh, shh, it's me, Detective Riggs." Goosebumps sprung up on every inch of skin.

Wait, how did he catch up to her so fast? He was on the other side of the house. Was he working with this other person?

He sat them both up then released his hand from her mouth and waist at the same time. Her eyes were wide, as the full moon cascaded down through the corn stalks.

"Miss Parker, I will not hurt you." He held his hands up. With his back turned to her he pulled his gun from his holster. Gun at eye level he spun in his knelt position and scanned the crops.

She pushed away from him, stood up, then took several steps back as tears from the adrenaline rush spilled down her face.

"He came in here after you. I lost sight of him but I thought if I was with you, he wouldn't try to come back for you."

"You're a part of this aren't you?" Kassidy hissed.

"What? No! What makes you think that?" Sawyer's brow furrowed as he shook his head.

"Why did you call me tonight and then come over?"

"Because I'm working on your case and you sounded upset on the phone."

"Who is in on this with you?"

"Look, Miss Parker, I'm not in on this at all. I called to check on you; to see if there was anything new. I am not a part of this. I'm trying to help you." Sawyer took a step toward her.

She stumbled back but caught herself before she fell.

Sawyer reached for her as she cried out and pulled farther away.

"Miss Parker, please trust me. I'm here to help you. Now, looking back about what has happened tonight, I can see why you would start to lean toward that way of thinking. However, please believe me: I would never do anything like this. I would never hurt you." His eyes pleaded with her.

Sirens approached as police lights reflected off the crops surrounding her and Sawyer.

Frantically, she looked from the lights back to Sawyer then back at the lights. Confusion clouded her thoughts. Why would he call for officers to back him up if he was in on it? On the other hand, had he done that to get the attention away from himself? She didn't know what to think when the officers yelled for Sawyer's location.

With his hand held up, he shouted back, "I'm over here." He lowered his hand to grab the flashlight out of his waistband then flashed it toward the house. Several officers crashed through the crops and joined them, guns drawn.

"Get her back to the house!" Sawyer barked.

"Ma'am, did you want to come with us?" The closest officer extended his hand.

Kassidy hesitated before she took it.

At the front door, she stopped dead. Sawyer and two other officers walked several paces behind, talking in hushed whispers on the way back to the house. Sawyer removed the gun from the back of his waistband again and the officers followed suit, drawing their guns. Two entered the house while one stayed with Kassidy and Sawyer. The alarm was silenced as the officer who had stayed with her turned it off.

She couldn't bring herself to look at Sawyer. She wanted so much to believe him but after tonight, doubt nagged in the back of her mind.

The two officers re-emerged from the house and nodded, but still Kassidy couldn't get her legs to cooperate to enter her house. One officer motioned for her to follow as he entered the house just in front of her. Kassidy walked with her back straight and stiff toward the kitchen and saw a rose on the counter. She spun on her heels. Sawyer didn't have time to stop before she walked right into his massive chest.

She struggled for breath and flinched when he put a hand on each shoulder and walked her around him. With guns drawn; they slowly entered the kitchen. Sawyer glanced over his shoulder and shook his head to Kassidy. She grazed his arm with her left hand as she reached around him and pointed to the rose on the counter.

An officer looked at Sawyer who only nodded at him. The officer picked up the rose and left the house. With a flick of his wrist, the evidence bag from the trunk snapped opened. Water droplets from the rose splattered the inside of the bag as it dropped into it.

"Now do you believe me?" Kassidy turned toward Officer Huffman.

"Yes, ma'am." He busied himself by writing in his notebook.

"The name is Kassidy," she snapped.

"I want a twenty-four-hour detail on this house. She had new locks installed today. I want to know how he's getting in here. This guy is serious and I don't want him to have any more access to her. He also called her today, so he's watching her." Sawyer's eyes locked onto hers.

She didn't say a word but walked down the hall to her office. She snatched the receipt the locksmith had given her and handed it to the officer closest to her. "This is the company I used. They promised me no one could pick this lock or bump the door open."

"These are the locks you got?" Sawyer peered over the officer's shoulder.

"Yes."

"These are excellent locks. Definitely one up on the recommendation list if I were to suggest anything."

Kassidy wasn't sure if that made her feel better or creeped her out more. There was still a knot when she thought about Sawyer being involved but it wasn't as intense as it had been earlier.

"Yeah, these are top of the line. There's no way he should be able to get past these." The officer looked at Sawyer.

"You thinking what I'm thinking?" Sawyer raised his eyebrows.

"What?"

"We think your guy may work for a locksmith. That's how he got around these new locks." Sawyer frowned.

"He isn't my guy!" Kassidy snapped. "How dare you!"

"No, I meant nothing by it. Miss Parker, please. I'm sorry that was a bad choice of words," Sawyer stammered. She could see Officer Martin's eyes were wide with shock as he stood behind Sawyer.

"If we're done for the night, I'm exhausted and would like to go to bed and try to sleep. Although I'm not sure I'll be able to."

"Yes, Miss Parker, we're done. Officer Martin, you'll have the first watch. You can type your report in the car. I'm going down to the station to get the schedule squared away. Don't handle any situation by yourself. If you see anything, call it in and wait for backup unless there's someone in this house besides Miss Parker."

Kassidy trudged over to the baseball bat she'd dropped in the front room earlier. She bent slightly at the waist to snatch it off the floor then brushed past the officer on the way back down the hall to her bedroom. She leaned the bat up against the bed where it would be easy to grab if she needed it.

"Miss Parker?" Sawyer asked from the doorway.

She spun around, grabbing for the bat.

"I'm sorry. I didn't mean to startle you. I want you to know I'm not involved. That isn't who I am or ever could be. I swore to protect citizens when I got this job and I've been doing it for fifteen years."

Kassidy slunk down to the end of the bed, while Sawyer talked. She glanced toward her bathroom. "Where's my toothbrush?"

The question was unexpected and Sawyer stared at her for a moment as if he wasn't sure how to respond. He slowly walked toward the bathroom door.

"I'm sorry I didn't mean to dismiss what you said." Kassidy stammered. "I want to believe you but I'm scared and this isn't something I understand or want in my life."

"No, I get that. You can ask me anything you want to know and I'll be one hundred percent honest with you. I've nothing to hide. Now, not to change the subject, but when was the last time you saw your toothbrush?" He continued into her bathroom.

"When I got home from dinner with my friends. I brushed my teeth then watched a movie before the phone call."

"Martin? Are you still in the house?" Sawyer yelled.

"Yeah, what's up, Detective?" Martin barely peeked around the corner.

"Please add in your report someone's taken Miss Parker's toothbrush."

"Her toothbrush, sir?"

"Yes, her toothbrush. Which part of that's hard to understand?"

"Yes sir, I'll add it to my report." Martin excused himself and left the master bedroom.

"Miss Parker?" Sawyer glanced at Kassidy.

"Yes?"

"I really need you to believe me. I have nothing to do with this. If you think I'm involved, it can only hurt the investigation. Because whether or not you believe it, you'll withhold information that could help catch this guy if you don't trust me." He stared at her intently, worry etched on his face. Lines creased his forehead and around his eyes as he studied her. It made him seem more human—not just a detective.

Silently she prayed for wisdom about what to believe. She met his eyes and suddenly all doubt was erased. He was no longer a threat. She trusted him completely. "I trust you."

"Good, now if you see anything at all—I don't care what it is—you call me on my personal cell, no matter the time. I'll have an officer stationed outside your house twenty-four hours a day for the next few days until we can figure a few things out. We'll follow up with the possibility he works for a locksmith and that's how he's getting in. We'll let you know what we find."

Sawyer handed her his business card. Her fingers brushed his as she took it. There was no fear when they touched. She ran her thumb over the added hand-written phone number indented in the back of the slick business card.

"Thanks. Don't think I'll sleep for a while. All I can see is him standing there and then grabbing me in my own house." A shudder ran down her spine.

"To be honest, I didn't like seeing him standing there and me not being able to get to you. It scared me." He diverted his eyes when she glanced up at him.

"I don't get it. I don't understand what I could've done to set him off."

"Sometimes you don't have to do anything. They are just wired wrong and the smallest thing sets them off. It's not anything that would put someone else in that frame of mind. They take it personally and think you meant something one way when actually it was just an innocent gesture."

"Well, thank you for being so honest. I think I'm okay. I'll just turn on all my alarms again to make sure he doesn't get the jump on me this time."

Her shoulders slumped, as her eyes started to droop. The corners of her room were now dark places for him to hide; she would leave all the lights on tonight.

"I'm serious: if anything happens, you call me. Let the officer know out back. If this guy gets in, you get out. I don't care how you do it, just get out of this house and run to the officer. I'd instruct you to get a gun for your protection but I have a feeling you wouldn't go for that, am I right?" Sawyer smiled and laughed. It was the first time she'd hear him laugh and she felt an attraction for him.

"No, I wouldn't." Nervous laughter filled the room; he only smiled wider.

"Well, lock up after me. Know your surroundings. Even the smallest feeling could be something with this guy." He strolled down the hall to the back door.

Kassidy followed him and he waited outside to make sure she locked the door and turned the alarm on. He smiled and offered a small wave as he strolled down the driveway toward his car.

With her back to the door, her house seemed to stretch in every direction. Every clock ticked loudly as if to block out any sound that would alert her to someone being in her house. A flash of his dark shadow grabbed for her. She shook her head. There was no way she would sleep tonight. She snatched the book she'd been reading.

A twist of the lock on her bedroom door felt flimsy, almost like a child's toy. Maybe a new lock on her bedroom door was in order. She wedged the chair under the door handle again then chuckled as she looked at it. She wasn't sure that would stop anyone. When she remembered what had happened the last time she'd pushed that chair in front of the door, she clutched her hands to her chest.

Kassidy pulled out her pajamas and ambled into her bathroom to brush her teeth again and get ready for bed. The plastic around her new toothbrush crinkled as she ripped it open. She flung her hand toward the trashcan, where the plastic floated halfway into the trashcan before it statically clung to the side.

Even with her teeth brushed to a shiny finish, she wasn't ready to settle in for the night. What if she fell asleep and he was there again when she woke up? Panic started to take hold.

She murmured a prayer under her breath for God to keep her safe and to let the police catch her stalker.

With all the lights on, she hauled herself into bed to read her book. About an hour later, she awoke with a start. Just as she feared she would, she'd fallen asleep. She listened with her breath held but heard nothing to alarm her. With a sigh, she untangled herself from her blankets. The legs of the chair bounced on the carpet as she dragged it away from the door. Her fuzzy slippers scuffed against the carpet as she shuffled to the kitchen.

Maybe her morning tea would wake her up. The spoon clinked against the delicate cup as she stirred in her milk and sugar. She was staring off into space when she saw movement out the back door. The cup shattered as it impacted with the cold tile floor and she let out a scream that sliced through the night's silence.

"Miss Parker?" Officer Martin drew his gun and then peered in through the back door.

"Officer Martin?" She had forgotten there was someone outside her house.

"Yes, ma'am. Are you okay?" He glanced around through the double paned glass on the door, but only saw Kassidy. Gun back in his holster he relaxed his shoulders.

"I'm sorry, I forgot you were out there. You startled me." She snatched a towel off the kitchen sink to mop up the floor.

"I'm sorry about that. I was just walking around the house to make sure it's still secure. Did you need anything?" His voice was raised so that she could hear him through the thick door that secured the back of the house.

Up on the tips of her toes, she switched the alarm off then opened the back door. "No thanks. Did you want something to drink? I could make you coffee. I don't drink it but my friends do."

"No ma'am, I have another officer bringing me an extra-large cup, so don't go to the trouble." He smiled.

"Okay. Hey, thanks for watching my house. It makes me feel a bit better knowing you're out there."

"Sure thing. Try to get some sleep; we'll have someone out here all night. I'm sorry again for scaring you." He stepped off the stairs then meandered back to his car, watching everything.

She locked the door and turned on the alarm. After she'd cleaned up her tea, she sighed. Maybe she *could* sleep now with the officer outside her house. Sleep sounded good, but she would still leave all the lights on. Her eyes drooped as she shuffled down the hallway to her room.

As she sank down under her thick heavy comforter, after locking the door and wedging the chair back under the doorknob, she slipped into a fitful sleep. Her mind wandered with thoughts of the stalker. Sleep was elusive as she drifted in and out of consciousness and tossed from side to side.

She forced herself to get up even though her eyes barely seemed to want to open. Her bed beckoned: the already toasty warm comforter and soft down pillow were inviting and almost succeeded in luring her back to their comforts. Instead, she grabbed her running gear and took it into the bathroom to change for her morning run. She snatched her brush off the cold, hard porcelain sink but her hand stopped halfway to her head. She struggled for breath. Her hair was a good six inches shorter than when she went to bed.

Seven

SHE RAN OUT OF THE bathroom and looked at the chair, still perfectly wedged under the doorknob of her locked bedroom door. A quick scan of her bed didn't reveal any hair from it being hacked off while she slept. She picked up her phone; her fingers trembled as she misdialed Detective Riggs' phone number. She hit end and tried again. Misdial. Her hands shook as she cleared out the number again. She slowed her breathing. With her eyes closed, she took in a breath then held it for several seconds before releasing it again. With the number finally typed in correctly, she almost cried out and raised the phone to her ear. Several rings in she held the phone away from her ear to make sure the phone number was right. It was. Another ring before he answered.

"Hello," came a groggy voice on the other end.

"Oh, I'm so sorry. What time is it?" Kassidy looked at the clock on her nightstand and saw it was only five am.

"Miss Parker?" Sawyer sounded more awake. "What happened?"

"He cut my hair." She couldn't stop the tears as she sobbed into the phone.

"I'm on my way over. Get out to the officer now and stay with him until I get there," Sawyer barked through the phone.

She yanked the chair back, unlocked her bedroom door, and bolted down the hall to the kitchen. Sock-footed she skidded to a stop halfway into the kitchen. A song she'd never heard before played on her stereo. With the crude lyrics, she knew she would never listen to that kind of music.

A knock at the back door made her jump. A different officer than Officer Martin stood there, with his gun in his hand. He wrapped his other hand firmly around the butt of the gun.

Kassidy moved quickly to the door and unlocked it for the officer. The alarm shrieked and made them both jump. Her clumsy fingers fumbled to try and shut off the alarm.

"Ma'am?" The officer looked young and she almost wondered if he was old enough to be an officer.

"He turned on my radio; it's playing in the living room. I never listen to that music." Kassidy waved her hand toward the living room as she scrunched up her face.

The officer motioned for her to stay where she was as he continued into the living room, gun raised. He walked back into the doorway of the kitchen and shook his head to let her know there was no one in the living room. He motioned that he would check the rest of the house and held up a hand telling her to stay where she was.

Kassidy had her back to the door when Sawyer pulled into the driveway. He got out of the car and stared at her for a split second.

"Miss Parker?" He asked as he approached her.

The young officer was back in the kitchen by now. He holstered his gun as he saw Detective Riggs. "The house is clear. No one in there, and no signs of forced entry."

"Officer, how did he get into the house?" Sawyer snapped.

"Sir, we were here all night. When she unlocked the door to let me in, the alarm sounded. There's no way he came in that door last night. We would have heard or seen something. We also walked the perimeter every half an hour as you suggested. He had to have been watching to know when to get in."

"Is that music?" Sawyer glanced to Kassidy.

"I didn't turn it on. I don't listen to that kind of music." Kassidy wrung her hands.

"Officer, check the outside again and see if he left any footprints. Anything, we can use to identify him."

"Yes, sir." The officer marched out the door.

"Now Miss Parker, you said he cut your hair?" The uneven ends were hard to miss.

"Yes, there isn't any hair on my bed or anything to show he cut it. It's just gone!" Kassidy broke down and sobbed.

SAWYER REACHED OUT for her but he didn't want to overstep the bounds with him being on the job. He quickly pulled his hand back. This was one of the worst cases of stalking he'd seen in such a small town. She'd already had the thought that he might be involved in this, which bothered him more than he wanted to admit. He didn't want her ever to fear him like that. It wasn't who he was. He refused to admit he had started to develop feelings toward her.

Her phone rang, and a look of pure terror crossed her face as her eyes widened. She reached across the counter and looked at the caller ID. He saw that she didn't relax when the caller ID showed Celeste's name.

"Hey, Celeste." She forced a smile at Sawyer as she walked into the front room, wiping the tears from her face.

Sawyer watched her, worried about what this guy would do next. He inspected the lock on the back door and saw no evidence that anyone had tampered with it. It was still unmarred from any use. This only added to his suspicions that the person responsible for the fear in this house, more than likely, worked for a locksmith.

The officer was back at the back door when Sawyer motioned him in. "Nothing, sir. There are no footprints, no pry marks, nothing."

"Okay, call into the station and have Huffman run a list of the local locksmith's around so we can run through employment records."

"Yes, sir." The officer shook his head. Sawyer saw him scrutinize everything he passed on the way to his patrol car. He knew if this had happened on his watch, he would be doing the same thing.

Kassidy walked back into the kitchen, phone in hand. "Celeste invited me over. I'll spend the day at her house after church."

"Good idea. I don't want you here if he can get around my officer and come in here unnoticed." Brow furrowed, Sawyer tried to work out who could be doing this. If he could just get his hands on this guy, he would feel much better.

"Do you go to church?" Kassidy asked.

"No, I don't really have time with work and all." A blush flushed his cheeks at the poor excuse.

"You should come some time. I think it would really help with your job. If you find the right church that teaches directly from the Bible and how it was meant to be taught, it'll change your world." Kassidy almost smiled.

"Thank you for the offer. I'll let you know. Did you want me to stay until you leave?"

"No, I think I'll be okay." She stared at him.

"Okay call if anything new comes up. I'll head to the station and get all this added to the report. We'll also look at locksmiths this week and see what we can find in employment records for them."

Sawyer let himself out. The sun was already bright on the horizon, announcing high temperatures for the day. He hoped she'd be okay.

"THANKS." KASSIDY LOCKED the door after him then hesitantly headed to her bedroom. She shuddered as she looked at her bed; at what could have been a terrible situation. What would have happened if she'd woken up while he cut her hair?

The absence of hair when she looked in the mirror made her want to cry all over again. A lump caught in the back of her throat and she forced herself to swallow past it. She wouldn't run today. She didn't like that he affected so many aspects of her life.

Back out of the shower in less than five minutes, she threw her hair up in a sloppy bun so no one would be able to see her cut hair until she could get in to her stylist. She haphazardly tossed clothes into an overnight bag, not caring that it bulged open at the top. She just wanted out of her house before the walls closed in on her.

Celeste and Henry would be more than happy to have her stay with them. Her only worry was that he would follow her to their house and hurt them.

Eight

"I WANT HER. I DON'T understand why I can't have her. Why won't she stop and talk when she's on her run?" He paced with short determined steps.

"I can help you get her." The voice was calm and gentle.

"How?" He stopped.

"Let me in and I can assist you," it reasoned.

"Let you in? But you're already *here*."

"I'm without a body. I require you to invite me in so I can assist you to acquire the girl."

"What are you?" His palms began to sweat as he thought about watching her run. He unconsciously wiped them on his jeans.

"I'm an angel," it cooed.

"But I'm confused. Why do you need me to invite you in to help me get the girl?"

"I can't assist you in this form. I must procure a body to do anything."

"Why can't you take another body and then help me?" he nodded.

"Because I'm only allowed to do what the person, whose body I'm in, requests me to do. I'm unable to occupy a different body and then perform tasks you ask of me." Its logic was sound.

"Well, that makes sense but I still don't know." He'd never needed help before when he wanted a girl. Crooked yellow teeth showed as he smiled at the thought of his other girls.

"What don't you know? I'm here, aren't I? You can hear me plain as day. Angels help people; we don't harm them."

"Will I have control of my body and my thoughts?"

"We don't do anything you don't want us to do—that goes against all of our laws. It is forbidden for an angel to harm a human or let them be harmed by our actions."

"I don't know. I want to think about it."

"Oh, absolutely; you can contemplate your decision, but know that Detective seems to be getting very comfortable with her and lately, he seems to be with her continually."

"Yeah, but it's only after we've been there. If I can get her then he won't need to be there anymore. She needs time to get to know me."

A police department had never interfered like this, making his prize so much harder to obtain.

"It's your decision and I can't formulate the answer for you. Just know you will suffer defeat in your pursuit of her if you don't get my help," it chided.

"Leave me alone for a minute, will you. I need time to think!"

Quick steps led him to the wall in the living room where he spun on his heels then marched to the opposite wall. He didn't know what to do. He liked her more than he had liked all the other girls. She was special to him. She smiled and waved back when she ran past his house. Yes, he wanted her, but he wouldn't let that voice in unless it was the last option. He could do this on his own; he really could. People never gave him the credit he deserved. Look how he got into her house even when she had those locks changed. His smile showed his crooked, ill-placed teeth. He was proud of himself for being so smart.

Maybe he could get her by himself, just maybe. What would he need to do next? He spilled coffee grounds on the counter as he made himself a cup of coffee. Either way, he would get her. None of the other girls were like her. There was something special about her; he couldn't quite put a finger on what was different.

That detective made him mad. Why did Mr. Detective have to show up all the time as if he was her knight in shining armor? That was *his* job, not that stupid detective's. He twirled a finger in the grounds that lay on the counter. He'd almost had her when she'd run into the field but then the detective had to ruin everything by being faster than he was. He slammed his fist onto the counter making the miniscule coffee grounds dance. He would have to take him out of the equation so he wouldn't hinder his plans for her. She would be his forever and no one would stop him this time.

"You will not obtain her without my collaboration." The voice interrupted his thoughts.

"Yes, I will. She'll be mine. You watch; she will." He knew he could do it. He had done it numerous times before.

"How are you going to get her? You've spent months surveilling her and you're no nearer now than you were when you initially saw her. You've never endured this long to seize a girl," the voice reasoned.

"I don't know. I know I want her though. She's mine."

"I promise we'll get her collectively; then you can spend the rest of your life demonstrating to her how much she means to you and see if she'll return the affections. Don't you want that? Have her reciprocate your feelings?" the voice soothed.

"Yes, I want that. She's amazing."

"You know the Detective's getting closer and closer to her. Did you see the way he ogled her through the door when you virtually obtained her the other night?"

"Yes." He clenched his fists and drove his fingernails into his palms. Indentions from his nails showed when he unclenched his fists just before the nails could break the calloused surface of his rough hands.

"He'll steal her from you. We must work collectively on this. You know they say two heads are better than one. Well, imagine your wants and desires with my capability to make them happen." The voice worked its magic as if it were a salesman trying to get the customer to agree to its terms on a contract.

"He can't have her. I saw her first!" Animated, Tucker slammed his coffee cup down on the counter.

Coffee sloshed out of the cup over the rim and mixed with the already spilled grounds. Sludge formed from the mixture of the two. Just because the last girls didn't work out, and he'd had to get rid of them, didn't mean this one wouldn't. She was different. No detective would take her away. He was superb at getting rid of men in the lives of the women who were special to him. He could get rid of this one as well.

"We must proceed now. We have to act decisively and procure her before he can."

Why did the voice make so much sense now? Would it be that bad to let it in just for a bit? Then, once he had the girl, he would tell it to leave. What could a voice do, really? He could handle it. He was stronger than some stupid voice. The thought of Kassidy being with him so he could teach her to like him, pushed him over the edge.

"Yes, I'll do it. But promise me: I get to tell you when to leave so it's just me and her." He was as giddy as a child on Christmas morning, jumping up and down.

"Oh, absolutely!" the voice growled.

He caressed the soft hair he held in his hand. The hair he had slowly and methodically cut so he didn't wake her rested in his calloused palm. He was ready. "Yes, you can come in."

Pain tore at his body as he screamed and contorted this way and that. The voice cackled and took over every corner of his mind, intentionally causing anguish until no thought was his own.

"Stop! What are you doing?" He doubled over as his knees slammed into the carpet.

"You permitted me in; now you're mine to do with as I choose." The sinister voice took on a malicious persona. The voice had a darkness to it as if it sucked the light out of the room just by speaking.

"You said you were an angel!" he screamed as he curled into the fetal position on the rough carpet.

"Angel, demon, you know, either one you decide," it howled.

"Nooo!" Blackness engulfed him.

Several hours later, still in pain, he awoke. Realization swept over him that he was no longer on the ground, but also not in control. It had cleaned up the coffee he spilled when he slammed his cup onto the counter. The hair was neatly bound in a tiny rubber band and braided.

"Oh, look who's finally roused." It knew it had control and didn't hide what it was anymore.

His house was cleaner than he had ever had it. The coffee table didn't have a speck of dust on it. Even the windows seemed to let so much more light in, with the layer of film that had built up over time, cleaned off. The glass globes around the lights shimmered.

"Come on, we require to go to the exceptional room. I want to affix the hair to our little compilation." It moved his feet without his approval.

"Why don't I have control of my body?" He fought to try and take back control.

"You invited me in. I can command whatever I desire to."

"But you promised I would get her; that she'd be mine." His heart soared as he thought of her and he was elated to find his feelings were still intact and his desire for her had not diminished.

"Oh, you will; you undeniably will. But I'm accelerating the timetable. We need to acquire her now. The sooner the better before that detective renders it unmanageable to get to her. What do you say? Are you prepared to do this?" the voice crooned.

"What? Right now?" His heart raced with nervous energy. What would she think? Would she be impressed that he knew so much about her? The thought of her being his was so exciting.

"Yes, now let me ponder a couple of things. We'll acquire her tonight."

The voice took over again, as Tucker faded to the back. Fog enveloped him and tried to block out his thoughts. He would focus on Kassidy—maybe his love for her would help him break free.

Nine

"THIS IS THE ENTIRE list of locksmiths in the area? I wouldn't call three, a list." Sawyer wasn't impressed.

"That's it. I can have the surrounding areas also checked. But that's all we have here in New Kingdom." Huffman kicked his feet up onto the desk and leaned back.

"Well, can we get a hold of them on a Sunday and get a list of employees? If we could get through the list today, that'd really help."

"Sure. Bob's is easy enough. It's him and his two sons and they've been in New Kingdom pretty much forever. Everyone knows them."

"Okay, so are you saying they're out?" Sawyer peered at Huffman over the top of the paper he held.

"Yeah, I'd say so. They're pretty stand up guys. Always willing to help and they have the contract with the department for our building and the security system here." Huffman grew up in New Kingdom and knew almost everyone who lived in it.

"Yeah, let's look at them as a last resort. What about the other two? Do you know them?" Sawyer looked to his officers for help, especially if they were as knowledgeable about the town as Huffman was.

"Well, I'd say Pat would be more than happy to give us his list. I can call him. The third one? Naw, it's new enough I don't really know 'em. We should have a contact in our business listings for after-hours situations." Heavy fingers pounded away at the keyboard to access the list.

A few moments later, Huffman was on the phone with Pat. He furiously wrote down a list of employees while Sawyer called the other locksmith from the number in the computer.

"Here's the list for Pat's." Huffman handed a list to Sawyer that was comprised of four names.

"Mr. Owens, this is Detective Riggs with New Kingdom Police Department. I was wondering if you could help us with a case we're working." Sawyer took the list from Huffman.

"I was wondering if I could get a list of your employees. No sir. We don't have a warrant. I was just wondering if you could help the police department. Yes, sir, I'll give you any information regarding your employees if I find anything wrong. Thank you, sir." Sawyer snapped his fingers to Huffman and wrote in the air with his pen. Huffman handed Sawyer the notepad he had snatched when he called Pat. Sawyer scribbled down a few names, thanked the owner, and hung up.

"Well, he almost didn't sound police-friendly." Huffman leaned against the doorframe that led to their small kitchenette.

"Yeah, he didn't want to get involved but on the other side he wanted to know if any of his employees were of the suspicious nature, since his insurance on his employees' hinges on them not being criminals." Sawyer glanced between both lists. Their list of only nine names, between the two companies, didn't look promising.

"Well, if these don't pan out, I betcha I can guess what I'll be doing this week." Huffman scoffed.

"Yes, you can. Do you know anything about these people?" Sawyer scanned the names and hoped that intuition would kick in, to tell him which one of them they wanted.

"Not really, I mean the owner at Pat's probably knows them well enough. He's a good enough guy; been in the business for near close to forty years." Huffman took Sawyer's list out of his hand to peruse.

"Forty years? That's a long time." Sawyer knew he could cross that name off his list. If he was the type to stalk, he would've had complaints on him by now and they would have had a case or two.

"Yeah, inherited it from his dad. I don't think he's the one for this. He's happily married and goes to that one church that's still open in town."

"Yeah, Miss Parker said she'd go to church today and then would spend the day with her friends. I wish there was a way we could know how this guy is getting in and moving around so well in her house. It makes you think, doesn't it?"

"Think what?"

"How long he's been doing this if he knows her house so well. He knows where everything is and when she got the door alarms and new locks." An overwhelming sense of dread flooded his thoughts.

"Yeah, I'm kinda sorry I said the things I did. I really thought she'd turn into one of our frequent fliers." Huffman made his way to the coffee machine and poured himself a steaming hot cup that was too hot to drink.

"Yeah, but I think it could have easily turned that way. She could have put those dishes out herself, and cut her own hair. When he grabbed her the other night...that still sends chills down my spine." Frequent fliers were commonplace from the city he came from, so he couldn't fault Huffman for having that thought initially.

"Yeah, I know. But now how do we catch him? This is really messed up. She's got to be so scared. And the officer on duty last night didn't see anything? Did he fall asleep at all during his shift?" Huffman weighed all the possibilities.

"You and I both know Officer Mitchell isn't one to shirk his duties just to catch sleep while on duty. He swears he was awake and kept doing perimeter checks every half an hour. I even checked his report. He recorded the time with every perimeter check and the computer log backs up his claims." Sawyer knew the officer took his job seriously no matter what was assigned.

"Well, we better check into this list of possible suspects. Did you want me to take Pat's list? I can talk to him and see if anyone hits him wrong. Someone may be new enough; he may not know them."

"Yeah, that'd be great. I'll investigate these and see if anything jumps out from their background check. Then we can make house calls if you are up to the task." Sawyer smiled. He knew Huffman would rather be out on the streets than in the office.

"I'm there. Let me know what you find. I'll get back to you on my list." Huffman grabbed his coffee, dumped it in his travel mug, steam rising out of the top, then topped it off at the coffeepot on his way out of the door.

Sawyer stood and tilted his head to each side to stretch out his neck muscles as he walked to his office. It would be a long, tedious day. As he sat down at his desk, he turned on his computer. His fingers flew expertly over the keyboard for the log-in to the criminal database. Personally, he preferred to see their names without suspicious activity than to rely solely on the employer's impression of them. Since Huffman trusted Pat so well, he would let Huffman handle his list his way until they ran into a brick wall; then he would run those names too.

Halfway through his list of five people, he saw something that caught his attention. The guy was a Steve Handstone. He'd jumped states like someone on the run from something. He had traffic violations like those Sawyer had seldom seen, and he was even showing an expired restraining order that should have been cleared out of the system before now. His ex-girlfriend had filed for one on grounds he was following her and tracking her cell phone. Sawyer knew contacting that police department had to be a priority.

He wrote the name of the police department and continued his search of the last two names. Not much showed on them. Although, one had absolutely nothing! He couldn't even find a driver's license for him. How are you a locksmith without a valid driver's license? Tucker Miles was the name he stared at, and he lived close to Kassidy. He wrote down that address and the one for Steven Handstone. Those two were now at the top of his list.

Sawyer had gotten up to grab a bottle of water out of the fridge as Huffman strolled back into the office.

"Anything good on your end?" Sawyer asked as his head popped out from behind the wall that led to their small kitchen area.

"Nope. Pat ran detailed background checks on all his guys. Even showed me the reports he got from state patrol and what was on 'em. He keeps a tight ship and don't tolerate any problems with his guys. After too many complaints, they'll fire you. Pat's a good guy. I trust him." Huffman refilled his to-go mug that was now bone dry.

"How do you drink that much coffee? Is your stomach lead lined?" Sawyer could never stomach the stuff. He'd tried it when he was a young officer and worked the midnight shift. He didn't care what anyone said, a good adrenaline rush out-ranked coffee any day of the week.

"Nope, it runs in my veins." Huffman laughed. "Did you find anything good?"

"I've got two possibles. Here." He handed the paperwork to Huffman.

"So, this guy had a restraining order before?" Huffman waved the criminal history packets at Sawyer.

"Yep. I was going to call the department they issued it out of and see what they had on him. You came back before I could make the call."

"Okay, what's up with this guy? There's nothing here. You didn't even print a copy of his driver's license."

"I can't find one on him. Don't you think he needs one, if he's a locksmith, to drive to customers?"

"Yeah, that might be just a small issue, but he has nothing." Huffman tossed the packets back on his desk.

"Look at his address." Sawyer raised his eyebrow.

"Is this right?" Huffman snatched the paperwork off the desk as his work boots thudded onto the floor when he sat forward. "He lives that close?"

"Yup according to water utilities, he moved in about six months ago."

"I say he's the first one we pay a visit to." Huffman stood to his towering height of six foot three and snagged the keys to the car off his desk, where he'd casually tossed them when he came back into the station.

"Sounds good. Let's go say hi." Glad to finally do something, Sawyer felt as if they may have a chance to catch this guy.

Ten

"COME ON, WE HAVE TO go. I need you to wake up so you can be a part of this amazing scheme I have." The voice jerked him back to consciousness.

"What? Why do you keep taking control and not letting me know what's going on?" Tucker whined.

"Oh, compose yourself. This surpasses anything you could have conceived."

He grabbed the hair he had cut from Kassidy and shoved it in the back pocket of his jeans. He stopped dead in his tracks, with his hand poised over the doorknob to his front door. He saw a police car pull up in front of his house.

"What do we do?" Tucker whined.

"Quiet yourself. We haven't technically done anything yet. Did you leave any evidence when you were in her house?" the voice accused.

"No!" he yelled at the voice.

A loud knock silenced him. Feet planted in place, he wasn't sure if he should run or answer the door.

"New Kingdom Police!" Huffman pounded on the solid oak door, while Sawyer kept an eye on the sides of the house with his hand on the grip of his gun.

Tucker opened the door a crack then smiled at the officer. "Yes, can I help you?"

"We have some questions regarding a case we're working?" The hair stood up on Huffman's neck as he held back a shudder. He moved his hand to the grip of his gun.

Tucker saw the movement. He narrowed his eyes at Huffman.

"Well, I was getting ready to head out. Will it take long?" Tucker took a step back from the door.

Sawyer backed up Huffman. "No sir, we just have a couple of quick questions."

"Please wipe your feet on the rug." Tucker's smile showed his plaque-coated, crooked teeth.

"Sure, thanks for letting us talk to you today. We know it's a weekend." Sawyer and Huffman scrutinized the house; it was spotless.

"You have a nice home, Mr. Miles." Huffman took another step inside.

Tucker flinched ever so slightly and hoped the officer didn't see it. "Thank you. I'm sorry, what are your names?" Tucker took another step back but didn't offer to shake their hands.

"I'm Detective Riggs. This is Officer Huffman." Sawyer extended his hand; which Tucker shook generously.

"What can I help you with this morning?"

"We're working a case where someone broke into a house down the street and we wondered if you'd seen anything or anyone out of the ordinary in the area?"

They took out their pads of paper and a pen then nodded their heads in response to what he had to say.

"No, I can't say I have. I keep to myself here and like my peace and quiet." Tucker squinted back and forth between

Sawyer and Huffman. He didn't like them being so close to him, especially with what he had in his back pocket. He hooked his thumbs in his back pockets and stroked Kassidy's hair.

"If you can keep your hands out of your back pockets, please." Huffman's hand returned to his gun.

"Oh sure, sorry just a habit." A sloppy smile plastered his face.

"Well, anything, even the smallest detail, would really help." Sawyer watched his hands.

"Sorry I wish I had so I could help you guys out, but I really didn't see anything." Tucker took a step toward the door.

"You have a really clean house. Do you have a maid that comes in? Maybe they saw something?" Huffman suggested.

"Maid? Oh no, I can't afford that. I, uh keep it clean myself."

"Do you mind if we look around?" Sawyer asked.

"Am I under suspicion for something?" He shuffled from one foot to the next.

"No, we're just looking at different houses in the neighborhood to see if they have the same layout that the victim's house does, that's all. Do you mind?" Sawyer stepped toward the kitchen.

"Well, I really was on my way out the door. If I'm not a suspect then I'd like you to leave. I really have to go."

Tucker started to sweat.

The voice in his head screamed to calm down. The only evidence in this house was in his back pocket, so unless they asked to search him, he was fine. Tucker almost laughed and hid the smirk on his face.

"JUST A QUICK LOOK WOULDN'T hurt would it?" Sawyer raised his eyebrows.

"Well, sure if it will only take a minute." Tucker started to follow Sawyer.

"Huffman, can you keep Mr. Miles company while I take a quick look?" Sawyer raised his eyebrow a fraction, so only Huffman would see it.

"Sure." Huffman turned toward Tucker. "So, what you do for a living Mr. Miles?"

"What, oh um, I work for a locksmith in the area." Tucker watched Sawyer walk off down the hall and half listened to what Huffman asked. He took another step toward the hall.

"Do you have a driver's license?" Huffman held out his left hand as his right hand released the double lock on his holster with a press of his thumb and forefinger.

"Why do you need to see that?" Tucker starred at Huffman's extended hand, its palm up.

"Just so's I can get all the information correct in my report."

"Oh, well, I can give that to you." Tucker spouted off his name and date of birth as Sawyer rounded the corner and rejoined them in the front entryway of the house.

"Did ya see everything you needed to?" Huffman raised his chin to Sawyer.

"Yes, we can go. You have a good day Mr. Miles." Sawyer was the first one out the door with Huffman close behind.

"So? Anything?" Huffman asked quietly as they made their way back to the patrol car as he scribbled the information Tucker gave him on his notebook.

"Not a thing. I've never seen a man's house that clean, especially one who lived alone. There wasn't even trash in any of the trash cans in the entire house." Sawyer opened the passenger door, slid into the seat then closed the door behind him.

"Wait. No trash at all?"

"Not even a speck of dust. The trash cans looked new."

"Okay, that's a little ridiculous."

"You're telling me. Did you find out anything, while I searched his house?" Sawyer glanced over as Huffman pulled into the driveway to turn around.

"No, and he didn't offer his driver's license; just gave me the info on it." Huffman handed Sawyer the small spiral notebook he'd written it on.

While Huffman drove to Handstone's address, Sawyer punched in Tucker Miles' information into the computer to see if his birth date would help with the search.

"Anything?" Huffman glanced at the computer then back at the road.

"No, still nothing." Sawyer didn't like it.

Huffman pulled in front of Handstone's address. They both got out of the car at the moment Handstone pulled into his driveway.

Handstone eyed the officers as he got out of his car. "Can I help you?"

"Mr. Handstone?" Sawyer asked.

"Yeah, who's wantin' to know?" Handstone crossed his arms.

"Detective Sawyer and Officer Huffman with New Kingdom Police, sir."

"How can I help you?"

"Can we ask you a couple of questions regarding a case we're working?"

"Sure, do you mind if we head inside? I have horrible allergies this time of year and I always have to have the air on." Handstone trudged up the steps to his front door.

"We can do that." Sawyer trailed Handstone.

"What's the case? If it has anything to do with Marcy, I haven't called or talked to her in two years. Honest. I don't want nothin' to do with her after the stunt she pulled." His keys clattered across the table that was just inside the front door. He motioned for them to come in. Dust covered the bookshelves with movies just haphazardly thrown on them. Sawyer wondered if his allergies included dust.

"If you don't mind, can you tell us why she had a restraining order on you?"

"Yeah, she was mad. She caught me cheatin'. She jumped me one night. When I defended myself, she said I beat her up."

Handstone lumbered over to the refrigerator, grabbed a soda, and held it up to Huffman and Sawyer.

"Oh, no thanks. So, what became of the case?"

"Judge threw it out when they listened to all the messages she left on my voicemail, saying she's gonna make me pay. Guess it paid off to not get mad and erase them, with what she said on some of 'em. My lawyer was a great gal—she got the charges dropped so I moved here and haven't talked to Marcy since." Handstone plopped into the lazy boy that seemed to conform to his body from years of use.

"Well, we're working a case where a young female is being stalked here in New Kingdom. We think the person responsible works for a locksmith." Sawyer threw it all out on the table then waited for his reaction.

"Oh, wow that's a darn shame. I'd never hurt a girl or scare her. Marcy was a mistake but I still never physically hurt her. Yeah sure, I messed around behind her back and I regret that. I shoulda broken it off with her and left her instead of hurtin' her like that. What can I do to help?" Handstone looked them in the eyes. He was an open book.

"Just if you hear anything around work—you know, anyone talks or brags about it—don't confront them; call us immediately. We'd appreciate it." Sawyer offered him one of his business cards from his worn leather wallet.

"Sure thing. She hasn't been hurt has she? Because I don't like that one bit. My mama was hit by her second husband and I hated seeing that. Swore I'd never hit a woman." Handstone glanced down at the card he held between two fingers.

"Does anyone you work with strike you as someone who would be capable of doing this?"

"Nah, not that I can think of. I mean I don't really talk to them or hang out with anyone; you know. I keep my personal life separate from my work one," Handstone uttered.

"Well, if you think of anything, you call us. Please don't talk to anyone about this since it's an ongoing case."

"Oh yeah, I won't say nothin' but I'll keep my ears open for you guys." Handstone lumbered to the door then gave each a firm handshake as they left.

"Yeah, I don't think he's involved. Just in case, can you check with the judge that handled that case and see what they have to say? Then we can rule him out completely." Sawyer buckled his seat belt as Huffman pulled away from the curb. He was sure Handstone wasn't their guy. Especially with how open he was about what had happened in the past. His mind shifted back to Tucker Miles' house and the eerie feeling he had when he stood near him. His answers to their questions had been too short and he'd wanted them out of the house too quickly.

Sawyer wanted this solved. He wanted to figure out what had started this and why it was happening. How could someone do this to another human being and terrorize them like this? He didn't know what made a person think this was okay or even want to do it. A lot of what he saw in his job shocked him, but some things particularly unnerved him. He often wondered what the world was coming to. He wasn't sure he wanted to continue doing this job with all the evil he saw in the world. But, who else would do it? Who would keep people safe and do what he did? Today's world got darker with each passing day and no one wanted to help protect and to serve.

He could remember when he'd started out, how there had been so many people who applied to be an officer he'd had to fight for his job. Now you couldn't find anyone who wanted to be an officer much less work for a living anymore. Deep down he knew he would stick it out until he physically couldn't do the job anymore. He felt he was in this job for a reason and it was something he'd always felt strongly about. He couldn't imagine doing anything else. Even with all he dealt with, which was nothing compared to the larger cities, he loved what he did.

Eleven

KASSIDY SAT STRAIGHT up in bed. Did she just hear a noise? There it was again! A loud scraping noise came from down the hall. Then silence. There it was again, so loud it echoed off the walls. It sounded as if someone was moving a chair, its legs scraping across the tiled kitchen floor with slight thumps as it hit the grouted areas. Maybe coming home after being at Celeste and Henry's all week was a mistake. Should she have spent another night at their place? She'd only been back in her home for a few hours.

Kassidy reached for her cell phone. Her heart raced when her hand landed on the hard wood of the nightstand where she'd left the phone. She knew she'd plugged it in to charge before she went to sleep. It was part of her nightly ritual before going to bed. She never forgot.

"Kassidy," a raspy voice called out from the darkness.

Kassidy leaped out of bed and stood there. Goosebumps covered her skin. Her breathing picked up as she gasped to pull air into her lungs.

He slunk down the hallway toward her room and blended in with the shadows. "Kassidy!" A man's voice cackled.

Kassidy hurdled the end of her bed then slammed her bedroom door. The flimsy, pathetic lock would be no match for this person. She ran to the other side of her armoire, which stood against the wall next to her door. She threw her shoulder against it and pushed with all her might.

Sudden thunderous knocks rattled the door, making her cry out, as her heart pounded in her chest. The sinister laugh from the hall sounded as if the man had his mouth pressed up against the door on the other side.

She slid down several inches with her back to the armoire and shoved with her legs. It moved a few inches, but it was too little too late. Her door frame gave way with an earth-shattering crash as the door flew open. The frame shattered, sending splinters flying everywhere into the room.

Kassidy was cornered! A dark figure loomed in the doorway. He continued to laugh hysterically as she weighed her options. Which, as she had to admit, were few.

Her heart sank as several thoughts ran through her mind of what he would do. She stepped quickly over to her left and put the bed between her and the intruder. He countered, also sidestepping quickly, so he was straight across from her when she saw who it was. The air rushed out of her lungs as her heart dropped in her chest.

Kassidy's voice cracked. "Tucker?"

Tucker lived in the neighborhood a few streets over. She would always wave if he happened to be outside when she ran, but that was it. She'd never even talked to him before but had heard his name from his neighbors who went to her church. Had he been the one this whole time breaking into her house and doing all of this?

"Yeah." His guttural laughter filled the quiet room.

"Tucker, we can talk you know. I can get us something to drink and we can sit down in the kitchen or on the porch and talk." Kassidy almost got the entire sentence out before her voice wavered and cracked again. She clenched her fists.

"You're right; we do need to talk, but not here. The cop outside would interrupt us. How about we go someplace quiet where no one can bother us?" Tucker held out his hand.

She shook her head. Where would he want to take her? Was he going to kill her? Kassidy closed her eyes and muttered to herself, "My God is stronger than yours."

"No. He. Isn't." Spit flew from his mouth as he screamed.

She flinched and shrunk away from him.

Tucker took a step up onto the bed. She was ready to make a run for it with a couple of quick steps toward the foot of the bed, but he reached out and snatched a handful of hair, yanking her off her feet. She scrambled to get her feet under her.

As she started to fall, he hooked his arm around her neck. He pulled her up to him and she felt him squeeze. She hit his arm then tried to claw at it. Tears streamed down her face as the room went dark. Just before everything went black, she heard him inhale deeply as he pulled her close with the arm he'd snaked around her waist.

"I LOVE THE SMELL OF your hair." Tucker felt her go limp and swept her fully up into his arms. He held her close and rocked her for several seconds. He couldn't believe he finally had her in his arms.

"Oh Kassidy, you will see how perfect we can be together." He smiled as he turned down the hallway with darkness in his eyes—there was nothing but pure hate and evil.

"You won't get a chance to see, Tucker; she's mine." Tucker's voice was dark and sinister.

Tucker shook his head and his eyes cleared slightly. "Yes, I will. You'll see. I want her to be mine."

An evil laugh echoed hauntingly down the hall, as Tucker's eyes faded to black. He tried to shake the voice away, but the fog took over and he was unable to do anything about it.

He hunched his shoulders against the cool breeze that came off the fields, as he pulled Kassidy closer. Tucker was a man possessed. He looked every which way, paranoid that someone would see him carrying his new prize. He darted through yards and between hedges to a tree line. As he ducked inside the row of trees, branches grabbed at him.

The officer on the back side of the house had just emerged around the corner to check the perimeter, but Tucker and Kassidy were out of sight before he had a chance to catch a glimpse of them. Tucker sneered in satisfaction.

Twelve

THE OFFICER ON DUTY saw the front door wide open and pulled his gun from his holster as he grabbed for his radio. Gun pointed at the front door, he quickly relayed to dispatch his need for more officers and to contact Detective Riggs. He swept around 180 degrees then turned back to the front door that showed only a dark hollow entry to a house with no signs of life.

The officer patiently waited for his backup to arrive on-scene and meet him at the front of the house. He nodded to his backing officer who grabbed his flashlight as he approached. Both officers entered the dark confines of the house, their flashlights dispelling any darkness as they swept across the rooms. From one room to the next, guns drawn, they were ready for whatever lay ahead of them.

SAWYER WAS IN HIS KITCHEN when his radio went off with the information from the officer who was at Kassidy's house. He grabbed his keys and practically ran out of the house, skipping several steps as he sprinted down to his car. He hit the remote start as he climbed behind the wheel.

Lights and sirens alerted the neighbors as he spun his tires and raced to Kassidy's house. His heart was in his throat at the prospect of what they would find this time. An iron grip on the steering wheel turned his knuckles white.

Sawyer slid into the driveway and barely missed the two marked patrol cars. He ran to the house and tried the back door. It was locked. He raced to the front of the house where he pulled his weapon as he approached the open front door and yelled, "Detective Riggs entering!"

"We're in the master bedroom. The rest of the house is clear," the officers yelled back.

Sawyer's heart dropped as he made his way toward the master bedroom, the light illuminating his way. He silently prayed that Kassidy wasn't dead. He paused; he couldn't remember the last time he'd said a prayer under his breath as he walked into a police situation.

Gun holstered and flashlight clipped onto his belt, he inspected the splintered doorframe. The indentions in the carpet from the attempt to move the armoire caught his eye.

His eyes searched frantically for Kassidy. "She isn't here?"

"No, I was doing my perimeter check and found the front door open. I didn't hear anything, and the alarm wasn't sounding. I immediately radioed in for backup and for someone to contact you." The officer snapped several pictures with the camera from the trunk of his patrol car.

"How's he getting around us?" Sawyer spat. A quick look around told him how scared she must have been, which only fueled his anger. "Check the area; I want the entire neighborhood locked down."

TUCKER HAD PLANNED this during the week she was at her friends. He could finally claim his prize. His Kassidy.

"She's not yours, she's mine." The evil voice sing-songed to Tucker.

"No, she's mine! I took all the risks!" Tucker almost yelled.

Its laugh was menacing when it was in control; it scared him, and it seemed to be in control progressively more and more. At first, it wasn't so bad: the entity had promised to help him get her, so he'd held onto that because that was what he wanted more than anything else. But now he wasn't in control at all. Now he had to fight to have even a few moments of clarity.

This one was one he would fight for though. This was a fight for his Kassidy. He saw her the first time she jogged by his house after he moved in. She waved and smiled. He knew in that instant that she was the one. She was so beautiful...and she'd waved at him! Not someone standing near him, but *him*. There was no one else in the world for him; he knew that now. Yes, there had been others. He'd had to run and move away because of them, but he could tell this one would be different. She wouldn't reject him as the others had. Oh, the horrible things he'd had to do to get them to love him, but in the end, they weren't good enough for him. He saw that now that he'd found his Kassidy.

A boring black sedan hidden in the row of trees was his escape. He fumbled to get the keys out of his pocket so he could open the trunk. He couldn't take the chance that someone would see her in the back seat or that she would wake up during the drive to his sanctuary. He cursed himself for not having the keys out before he carried her all the way to the car.

He used the trunk to prop her against with her head resting on his shoulder. He tightened his grip on her so he could get the keys out and open the trunk. The light seemed so bright at this time of night, it glared out of the trunk opening like a beacon telling everyone where he was. He would have to hurry so the brightness wouldn't bring unwanted attention.

Tucker gently placed Kassidy in the trunk on top of a sleeping bag. He then covered her with a blanket he had put in the trunk just for the occasion. It was one he had taken from her house. He wanted her to be comfortable. He'd had to wait the week she'd spent at her friend's house until she came home. The wait had felt like an eternity. He would now take such great care of her. He knew it. She would learn to love him and they would be the happiest couple. Everyone would be jealous of him, that he had her all to himself.

Tires spun on the dirt as he rocketed out of the grove of trees, down the road to their new home. He had the perfect place for her and no one would ever guess where it was. It was ideal. He'd found it months ago, and no one was the wiser. Since he'd spent so much time there lately, he felt his job would soon get in the way. He would quit soon enough so he didn't worry about it.

A police car approached with just the emergency lights on but no sirens, and he tightened his grip on the steering wheel. Anxiously, he watched in his rearview mirror as it continued into the darkness until all he could see were the flashing lights alerting anyone to the police car's location. He continued down the road, ready to ditch the car if the officer turned around. He didn't, so Tucker kept going.

SAWYER NOTICED THAT Officer Huffman had joined them in the doorway to Kassidy's room and nodded to Sawyer that he had something.

"Martin saw a car leave the wooded area on the way here. Only saw a driver in the vehicle. Martin is outside checking the exterior for evidence."

"What direction was the car headed?" Sawyer ran toward the front door with Huffman on his heels.

"West."

Thirteen

KASSIDY JOSTLED AROUND in the trunk and slowly came around. The brake lights illuminated the interior of the trunk well enough to know she was officially in over her head. "My God is stronger than his," she said to herself.

"No!" A scream erupted from the interior of the car. The car jerked from side to side and flung her from one side of the trunk to the other. She instinctively put her arms up to take the brunt of the impact as she was tossed from one side to the other. The coarse carpet rubbed roughly against her skin.

As the car's tires screeched to a stop, she thumped up against the back seat.

I wonder...

With as much conviction as she could, as the car took off at a high rate of speed and rolled her to the front of the trunk, she whispered, "My God is stronger than yours."

"No!" Again, screams from the interior of the car reached her in the trunk. This time the car made a wild turn and came to an abrupt stop, hurling her up against the back of the back seat.

The driver's door opened and a few milliseconds later the trunk lid opened. Tucker literally foamed at the mouth as his eyes pierced the trunk, searching for her. The hatred she could see in his eyes scared her to the core. But wait. Was there also a glimmer of fear?

"He isn't stronger than mine! I will show you! You will see and then admit you're wrong, little lady!" With that, he swung back and hit Kassidy right in the face.

Tucker slammed the trunk lid shut. A few seconds later the driver's door banged shut.

Kassidy saw stars as she gingerly touched her cheek. She closed her eyes as she cradled her cheek in her hand. She'd never been hit before. Was this what her aunt felt all those years with her abusive husband?

The car rocketed away at breakneck speed, giving her hope that an officer would notice and pull them over. At least she prayed for as much.

After several minutes, the car slowed down, dashing all hopes she'd had of the car being noticed as it raced down the road. It wasn't long after that, she felt them make a wide turn. Her feet braced on one side of the trunk and her arms on the opposite side kept her from rolling freely in the trunk. Now he backed the car up several feet before he turned off the engine. The engine started to tick as it cooled. The driver's door opened then closed. She didn't know what fate waited for her when the trunk opened and she would face Tucker again. It was a thought she didn't relish.

As the trunk lid opened, Kassidy's breath caught in her throat. Was this a school gymnasium? No, wait; it was a recreation room for one of the closed churches. But which one? Not as if that mattered. No one would show up for any service and come to her rescue.

Tucker offered her his hand to help her out of the trunk. She took it since she wasn't sure if it would set him off if she refused. His skin was cold to the touch and his callouses hurt her hand. The lights glinted off the chain on the doors. No one would stop to check on a car parked in an abandoned church parking lot either since he had driven it into the church rec room itself.

As soon as her feet were solidly planted, she let go of his hand. She fought the urge to run and put distance between her and Tucker. That would be futile since the room looked secure with no hope of escape.

Tucker seemed to get worked up as she let go of his hand. His face contorted as he looked down at his now empty hand. He slowly pulled out an enormous knife as a sinister smile crept across his face. He almost didn't look human. There was a hardness in his eyes, pure hatred, or was it something evil?

He pointed with the knife where he wanted her to go and as she turned in the direction he had motioned her, she saw another set of double doors. Back straight, she walked toward them. The distance seemed much farther than it was because of the knife. She came to peace with the fact that she probably wouldn't leave this church alive.

Echoes from their footsteps filled the eerily empty room where no doubt kids had laughed and played once. With what seemed to take an eternity, they reached the far end of the rec room. Tucker motioned for her to go through the doors. Kassidy pushed down on the push bar and took a tentative step forward. What would she find on the other side of the door?

Fourteen

SUN STREAMED THROUGH the stained-glass windows and splashed everything with brilliant colors. They had walked into the sanctuary. She couldn't help but feel close to God. Who wouldn't? It was breathtakingly beautiful.

Kassidy took in the whole room and while she took in its beauty, she also scanned for ways to escape. He placed his hand on her shoulder which caused her to flinch. Tucker snickered.

"So, is this where you imagined we would end up?" Tucker taunted.

"No. I can say, it wasn't even a thought."

The evil, sinister laughter was back, and it sent goosebumps down her arms. The door slammed shut behind them with a loud reverberating thud as he pushed her forward.

IN THE PASSENGER SEAT of Huffman's car, Sawyer scanned the area as they drove west and approached the grove of trees just past Kassidy's house.

"Stop!" Sawyer yelled, pointing and Huffman followed his gaze to the acceleration marks that came out of the trees and continued west on the pavement. Huffman shoved the accelerator to the floor on the police cruiser. The engine caught and propelled them forward as they left their own marks on the pavement.

Several miles further, Huffman slid to a stop on the lone deserted road as the sun crested over the horizon. He and Sawyer looked at each other then back at the marks that showed where a vehicle had stopped abruptly. They eyed the fresh marks then accelerated back down the road.

There wasn't much on the side of town where they drove to—just a couple of residences and an empty, closed church.

Huffman continued west to the church. As he turned into the parking lot on the back side of the building, he nodded to Sawyer.

Sawyer and Huffman stepped out of the police cruiser and unholstered their guns in a quick fluid motion as they approached the building. With a quick glance in the windows at the back of the church, they saw a vehicle parked in the gymnasium. Huffman radioed for backup and for the fire department to stage since they had no clue what they could walk into. The vehicle matched the description that Officer Martin had given Huffman.

Fifteen

THERE WEREN'T MANY pews left in the abandoned church's sanctuary. They had entered from the side and the emptiness made her sad. She hoped her church never saw the day where it closed its doors for good. Disturbed dust from where they walked floated in the rays of sun that penetrated the stained-glass windows.

"Oh, keep walking. I have a surprise for you." Tucker's voice wasn't his own, but rough and dark.

Kassidy did a quick scan of the sanctuary but didn't see anything out of the ordinary, except the lack of pews. She glanced back at him and then at the knife. She hoped the surprise didn't involve the knife. Her palms started to sweat.

"Keep walking." He pointed with the knife, which caught the sun and threw a reflection onto the wall. This time he wanted her to go across the rows, or where the aisles once were, on the other side of the sanctuary. She followed the indentions in the carpet which the pews would once have called home. The carpet was faded compared to the indentions where the pews had kept age from wreaking havoc on the fabric.

Carefully, she sidestepped her way between the few pews that were still there and slowly made her way across to the other side. As she stepped to where the outside aisle used to be, she saw her ‘surprise’. Her breath caught in her dry throat and she stifled a cough.

On the ground, halfway down the aisle, was a gruesome board with nails hammered through it as if it were an ancient torture device from medieval times. The nails were all different sizes, hammered in at all different angles. She spun her head in Tucker’s direction and she finally saw the evil that possessed him because no human could look that sinister. She wondered what kind of demon had taken control of him.

“I can tell it’s a surprise!” The demon clapped Tucker’s calloused hands as if it had just won a prize.

“My God is stronger than yours!” This time Kassidy had never meant it more. She knew who his god was—Lucifer—and she spoke to it, not Tucker.

“No!” It shook its head. It foamed at the mouth then lunged forward, slapping Kassidy across the cheek it had already hit when she was in the trunk. The blow threw her off balance but she caught herself on the cold, hard wall before she could land on the floor.

Her hand shook as she raised it to her cheek and felt warm blood trickle down it. She straightened back up and faced the thing again.

“So, you think you’re so smart, huh?” It grinned and seemed to revel in the fact it caused her pain. “You really think your God is stronger than mine?”

“Yes! You know it’s true!” She stated without hesitation before it could say anything else.

It flinched at her matter-of-fact comment. “You’re wrong!”

Next Tucker spoke. His eyes grew wide as he gawked at her cheek. He turned away from her and spat out, "You said we wouldn't hurt her!"

"Tucker?" Kassidy had to get through to him.

He turned to face her and she could see sadness fill his eyes. "I'm sorry. It said it would help me get you, so you could be all mine. I wanted to show you how great we could be together."

"Tucker, you could have talked to me." Kassidy forced a smile she hoped he would think was genuine.

"No, he couldn't; you wouldn't have taken the time of day to get to know him," it spat out and she realized she had lost Tucker. The demon was back in control. "Move!" Foam seeped out of the corner of its mouth as it smiled then pointed to the board with the knife.

So many thoughts rushed through her head as she tried to think of what she could do to get Tucker back so that maybe this could end.

"Kneel to me."

"No." She squared her shoulders, ready for it to lash out again. She was ready to die for her God and her King.

"Kneel to me and my god." The sneer disappeared as if it tired of her.

"No, I only kneel to the one true God, and He's stronger than yours." Her voice was strong. She knew it was her personal Savior Jesus Christ who had died for her, wiping her slate clean.

"Oh! You only kneel to your God. Oh! Well, I say we have a dilemma then!" It pranced around her.

It looked down at the board with the nails and played with the knife. Kassidy wished it would just put the knife away. She didn't dare try anything while it still held it.

"Well, I guess one way to solve our little problem is to see how devoted you are to 'your' God. Let's see, you can either kneel to me or you can kneel to your God." With that, it pointed to the wooden cross that still hung at the front of the sanctuary draped with beautiful purple fabric that had faded with a collection of dust from the closed empty church.

With her back turned, she started to kneel facing the cross and she knew this was probably the end. She didn't care. She could find no better way to die than to die for her personal Savior. She also knew what awaited her in Heaven if she died for Jesus. There would be a martyr's crown. A smile played at the corner of her mouth. She didn't care. She would die for her King no matter what it did to her.

"No!" It screamed as Kassidy flinched. "You didn't let me finish with the rules first. If you kneel to your God, you must kneel on the board. Or you can save yourself all that pain and suffering and kneel to me and my god." It spread its arms wide as if to welcome home a lost child. "Oh, and one more thing. If you refuse to kneel, then well, I must use this." It smiled at the knife it seemed to hold so delicately now, as if it was a fragile trinket.

"I will never kneel to you or anyone else. There's only one true God and that's my God who sent His son to die for me." Kassidy shook as she turned her back. She waited for it to plunge the knife into her back. Tears streamed down her face but she never took her eyes off the cross. She would be strong for her Father in Heaven, as His son was strong for her when he became the perfect sacrifice, even though fear shook her to the core.

It grabbed a handful of hair and yanked her forward making her stumble. It kept her off balance and maneuvered her toward the board until her toes kicked the edge.

"Last chance. Kneel to me Kassidy and I can make this all go away," it whispered, almost gently, into her ear while it still held a handful of hair.

"My God is stronger than yours." That was all she could say when its hand that had her hair thrust her forward and made her almost fall onto the board. It yanked up at the last second to keep her hands from stopping her fall as her shins hit first, followed by her knees.

A cry escaped her as the first nail punctured her skin, digging deep. It let go of her hair as it squealed in delight. But delight quickly turned to anger as it realized it had just lost yet again to faith and belief in the scriptures and promise of everlasting life from the perfect ultimate sacrifice.

It pushed with all its might and shoved Kassidy forward as the last part of her legs made full contact with the nails. Several more punctured her legs and knees as she cried out in pain. Tears splashed onto the board but were quickly absorbed by the dry splintered wood.

It stormed off down the aisle then yelled back over its shoulder. "If you get up, you die!"

SAWYER AND HUFFMAN continued their exterior search of the church. They only took a split second to glance in each window as they maneuvered around to the front. Their top priority was to Kassidy and her safety. They looked at each other as they heard yelling come from inside.

They crept up to peer into the sanctuary's stained-glass windows. Sawyer found a pane that had a clear piece of glass and observed Tucker Miles inside with his enormous knife. He motioned Huffman over, who also glanced in through the window.

"Do you see Miss Parker?"

"Look past the pews on the far side, you can just see the top of her head."

Sawyer peered through the window again. "Okay, that doesn't look good. Why is she like that?" Sawyer heard cars pull into the parking lot. He motioned to the additional officers where to park, then to meet him at the front of the church.

Huffman and Sawyer jogged to the front doors and noticed the chain through the glass around the push bar handles of the door that locked it in place.

Sawyer pushed on the door quietly. The door opened enough to show that they weren't locked by the deadbolt, just the chain. As the fire department pulled into the parking lot, Officer Martin was the first to round the corner of the building with three more officers in tow.

"Martin, grab bolt cutters from fire." Sawyer looked through the doors at the front entrance of the church and saw the double doors to the sanctuary just through a large doorway to the right of where they stood. He pointed them out to Huffman who nodded.

Martin sprinted back over as Sawyer pushed the doors open just enough for the bolt cutters to fit through to cut the chain. Martin applied ample pressure on the handles and cut the chain easily. Huffman quickly caught the chain before it clattered to the ground, making almost no noise. He placed it on the overgrown bushes by the door then he grabbed his gun and raised it as he fell in line behind Sawyer and tapped his shoulder that they were ready to enter.

Two officers stayed outside. One on the front, while the other made his way toward the recreation entrance, to keep eyes on the car.

SILENTLY SHE PRAYED as she still looked at the cross. "Father, I need you now more than I've ever needed you. Please help me be strong. You are my God and my King. I give this to you because this is more than I can handle on my own."

"Kassidy, are you okay?" Tucker looked at her as tears filled his eyes.

She refused to take her eyes off the cross; it seemed to give her strength. Tucker had turned her world upside down. She no longer felt safe in her own home. How did this get so completely out of control? Would she live through today?

"My God is stronger than yours." She hadn't realized she'd said it out loud until Tucker responded.

"Shut up! It will hear you!" Tucker shouted.

Kassidy prayed as Tucker took a step closer. Tears splashed onto the board and mixed with the blood that pooled close to the jagged broken edges.

Tucker paced and argued with his inner demon. She didn't know what led him to invite such a despicable thing into his life. She couldn't help but pray for him; she couldn't imagine living a life without God in it—being susceptible to demon possession. What had happened in his life to bring him to this junction?

"Your God is nothing!" it hissed.

Kassidy finally raised her eyes. "God loves you, Tucker."

"Well, He apparently doesn't love you. Look at what He's making you go through!"

"God didn't do this, Tucker, you did. Don't blame God for your actions. It's called free will. He gives you the choice on how you live your life."

"Shut up!" Foam spilled out of his mouth and down his chin.

Kassidy dropped her head and went back to praying. She could feel God with her and with each exclamation of His love, the pain lessened. There was a warmth in her heart that seemed to spread down to her legs. She knew she would make it through this. Her God was stronger than his.

Tucker paced wildly again, a man possessed. Maybe that's what God had her here for—to help this lost soul.

Sixteen

KASSIDY SAW MOVEMENT out of the corner of her eye. She didn't look up but kept her head down. She didn't want Tucker to see her move, but since he was on her right that could only mean Sawyer had found her.

Sawyer was good at his job and lately, Kassidy saw him too often it seemed. However, he was a good detective and she was thankful for that today. Sawyer and three officers made it to her before Tucker noticed that he and Kassidy were no longer alone. He seemed so preoccupied with his inner battle and muttering to himself that when he finally saw the officers, they were next to Kassidy. She saw him raise the knife toward the officers just before Sawyer stepped in front of her and blocked her view of her abductor.

"DON'T DO IT, MAN. JUST drop the knife." Sawyer's voice echoed off the walls of the abandoned church.

Sawyer and three officers had their guns trained on Tucker. He saw the struggle on Tucker's face as he contemplated what he would do. Tucker took a step forward and Sawyer's finger moved to the trigger of his gun. He really didn't want to shoot Tucker but he wouldn't hesitate to do his job to keep them all safe. He'd seen what kind of damage could be done with a knife when an officer was hesitant to shoot a suspect.

"Oh look, Kassidy's hero, Detective Sawyer Riggs to her rescue," Tucker spat. He glared at Sawyer.

"Tucker, just drop the knife. There are four guns pointed at you. You can't win this. Put down the knife and we can talk." Sawyer still blocked Tucker's view of Kassidy.

"No! She's mine! I only want to talk to her!" Spit flew everywhere. "Just leave us alone. She needs to learn what we can be together. She doesn't see it yet but I can help her see it if you leave us alone and give me more time with her."

Tucker stepped over to see Kassidy. Sawyer met him step for step to block his view.

Sawyer took a step forward and Tucker glared at him with such pure hatred. Then his eyes seemed to turn black and Sawyer stopped mid-stride. The hair stood up on the back of his neck.

Tucker took a step back, turned, then made a mad dash for the choir doors behind the empty pulpit that had not heard a sermon for several months. He seemed to be arguing with himself as he disappeared into the darkness that swallowed him whole.

"Go after him!" Sawyer ordered the three officers. Each reached for their flashlights as they entered the dark cavernous doorway and disappeared after a madman.

Sawyer keyed up his radio and called for fire and paramedics—who had staged outside—that it was safe for them to enter.

"Kassidy?" Concern filled Sawyer's eyes when he finally saw what she knelt on. He tried to hide the anger he felt.

Tears overflowed as soon as her eyes met his. "My God is stronger than his."

The doors crashed open as paramedics and firefighters rushed into the room. They stopped dead in their tracks when they saw Kassidy's predicament.

"KASS?" HENRY TOOK A tentative step forward. Henry, who had been Kassidy's friend for as long as she could remember, was also a paramedic for the local fire department. Apparently, he was on duty today.

"Hey, Henry. You and Celeste have any plans this weekend? I was thinking of a cookout, maybe kabobs?" Kassidy's smile was playful but she knew he could see the fear and pain behind her eyes. They had known each other long enough that he would know the real Kassidy behind the false front she put up.

He ran over the rest of the way with his partner and firefighters close behind, urgency to reach his friend written all over his face. He knelt next to Kassidy, to get eye level with where the nails punctured her knees and shins. "That's a lot of nails."

"Gee, but they aren't in straight rows, kind of crooked. He could have made them better." Kassidy winced as she once again felt the nails' full force and whispered under her breath, "My God is stronger than his."

"Yes, He is Kass. Now let's see about getting you out of here and to the hospital." Henry looked at the firefighters who were also knelt on the other side of the board opposite Henry to assess what they would need in order to transport her immediately.

"Brandon, go grab the saw. Matt, grab the backboard, and let's get her stabilized." The two firefighters took off at a jog. They came back in shortly carrying what Henry had requested. In the meantime, Henry grabbed his 'first-in-kit' as he called it, pulled out the BP cuff, and recorded her vitals on his clipboard.

"Kass it'll be loud as we cut this board down to a size we can fit in the back of the ambulance," Henry explained as he took her pulse.

"Just get me off this thing!" she exclaimed as pain rushed through her legs. Fresh tears trekked down her already tear-stained face.

"I'm sorry but we don't know how deep they go or what kind of damage they may have done."

"No, get me off this thing now. I don't care just get me off of this." She tried to stand but Henry grabbed her left hand to stop her. Sawyer grabbed her other hand to help Henry.

Panic set in. All she knew was that the board hurt. Rapid, short breaths bounced off the walls as she started to hyperventilate. With a twist of her hands, she pushed up against Henry and Sawyer and started to lift herself off the board.

"Kass stop. You could do more harm if you remove yourself this way! I need you to calm down and take a slow breath for me." Henry tried to let go of her hand but she had it in a death grip.

"No, I have to get off this now. I can't do this anymore." Panic took over as she hyperventilated. Sawyer's muscles tensed as she tugged on his strong hands.

"Kassidy, look at me, you need to listen to Henry. Slow your breathing. Come on, you can do this. Come on, look at me." Sawyer squeezed her hand to try and keep her from using him to remove herself from the board.

"Kass, he's right. I understand you're scared and in pain. I can give you something to help." Henry tried to get Kassidy to look at him. "Josh, grab an IV."

With all her might, she gripped both their hands and yanked her legs up as she ripped them from the board. She cried out in agony as she freed herself from the torture she could no longer endure. The firefighters' mouths fell open as they got a full glimpse of the board. Sawyer swept her up in his arms before she collapsed. Gently he set her down on one of the few pews left in the church close by.

Henry and his partner grabbed rolls of gauze out of their first-in-kits and wrapped her legs, inspecting them for any excessive bleeding. Those they addressed with extra packing before they wrapped the gauze around the rest of her legs.

"Dang it Kass, I told you not to do that."

Kassidy felt like a mummy but continued to lean against Sawyer who supported her on the pew. Her eyelids felt heavy and they slowly closed. She was spent from her time on the board.

Henry finished the leg he worked on about the same time his partner Josh finished the one he worked on. There were spots of red that showed through the starch white gauze, but neither of them seemed overly concerned with what they saw as they started to get her ready for transport to the hospital. Josh started an IV.

Three officers appeared through the front door, sweaty and out of breath.

"Where's Tucker?" Sawyer snapped.

"Well, he's fast," Huffman replied.

"Well, he has to be to outrun you, Huffman." Sawyer meant it as a compliment. It was a well-known fact around town that no one could outrun Officer Huffman and if he was on duty, no one dared to try.

"He's still out there?" Kassidy's voice broke. Her heart raced at the thought of Tucker waiting for her at home. She didn't want to go through anything like today ever again. Her left hand clutched her chest. She hadn't felt dread like this since the police knocked on her door years ago to tell her about her parents.

Sawyer squeezed her shoulders. "Huffman get that board logged into evidence and get crime scene out here immediately. I also want this church checked, top to bottom. Call in County if you need help with the search. They're always itching for a good call. Call me if you find anything I need to know about."

Henry left then came back in with the stretcher as Sawyer picked her up. He tenderly placed her on the stretcher so he didn't jar her legs or pull her IV. Henry slung his first-in-kit over his shoulder then grabbed the edge of the stretcher. The hard-plastic buckles clicked as Josh fastened each strap, securing her to the stretcher. Echoes from the squeaky wheels bounced off the walls of the abandoned church.

"Riding with or following?" Henry looked at Sawyer who was at the foot of the stretcher to help to guide it through the doors.

"Following, unless you need me to ride with."

"No. Following is fine." Henry hopped into the back of the ambulance and guided the stretcher in as Josh loaded it, closed the doors, then jogged around to the front to climb behind the wheel. Henry checked her vitals and rechecked her bandaged legs. He added more tape to her IV.

SAWYER'S PHONE RANG and as he listened, he hung his head. He opened the back doors to the ambulance and held up his index finger to Henry.

He continued his conversation in a cryptic whisper with his back turned to them. "Are you sure I need to see this? I'd prefer not to leave her without an officer with her. Fine. Okay!"

Sawyer glanced at Kassidy over his shoulder. With a furrowed brow, he turned back toward Henry. Sawyer closed his old antique flip phone, which people always teased him for.

"What's wrong?"

"Not sure yet. They need me inside. The officers say they've found something. Henry, I will have an officer meet you at the hospital. Don't leave her if he isn't there when you arrive. Don't stop for any reason on the way there. Miss Parker, I'll be there shortly."

Before anyone could respond, he slammed the doors of the ambulance. He took off at a jog then disappeared into the church. He forced himself not to look back in case he changed his mind. The edge in the officer's voice told him he needed to stay even though he couldn't ignore the fear in her eyes.

The last thing Sawyer heard before he walked back into the church was the ambulance kick up gravel as it left.

Seventeen

SAWYER STEPPED BACK into the church and marveled at how beautiful it was. Sun streamed through the stained-glass and splashed color everywhere. He could understand why people enjoyed attending a church. Peace flooded him when he entered through the doors as if all the worries of the world were insignificant. Even after the gruesome sight of Kassidy on the board, there was still calm in his heart.

An officer stepped through a doorway at the other end of the sanctuary and motioned for Sawyer. He glanced down at the blood-pooled board that Kassidy had knelt on and cringed. It now had a marker next to it for the photos taken, to log into evidence. He stiffly walked the length of the church. "What did you find?"

"This is the most messed up thing I've ever seen." The officer's voice was on edge.

Down a short rickety flight of stairs that creaked from the weight of the officers' thick-soled boots, they directed him to a doorway at the end of a hall where Huffman shook his head.

"Would someone tell me what's going on and why I left an unprotected victim to ride in an ambulance all the way across town?"

Officer Huffman sidestepped out of the way for Sawyer to enter the room. The long low-toned whistle echoed down the hallway as Sawyer froze. He stared into the room, unable to wrap his mind around what he saw.

There, on three walls, were hundreds of photos of Kassidy. Any photo with someone else in it, had that person's face slashed. Tucker had meticulously dissected other pictures so only Kassidy remained. Magazine photos of models in wedding dresses had Kassidy's head in place of the models'. On another wall, every picture had 'mine' scrawled in red across Kassidy and an X through anyone else in the picture with her.

Sawyer's eyes were glued to the photos. Of all the hundreds of photos, it didn't look like any two were the same. How many photos had he taken without her knowledge? For the first time in his life, he feared for someone's life, and it wasn't his own.

"Is this right? I don't see any that are the same." Sawyer spun to the other officers, who by the looks on their faces, had come to the same conclusion.

Some were taken at parks, others while she shopped, then even more when she ran in the neighborhood. The most disturbing ones, that shook him to his core, were the ones he had taken while she slept. This lunatic had a way into her house and Sawyer questioned how long he'd watched her. Kassidy was right: there had been someone in her house all those times she'd called.

Along the bottom of the pictures, he'd filled a shelf with several different items. Sawyer couldn't believe what he saw as he stepped closer. Trash, all kinds of trash: from chewing gum, which he would guess to be Kassidy's, to half-eaten food and even a toothbrush. His eyes locked onto strands of hair in a braid. He knew by the color, it was Kassidy's. He examined it without touching it.

Terrified and frantic one morning, Kassidy had called him. Someone had cut her hair while she slept. She'd told him she knew it was at least six inches shorter than when she went to sleep the night before. Nevertheless, they hadn't found any hair on her bed or pillows to show that anyone had cut it. Tucker had methodically taken every piece of hair with him.

All Sawyer could do was shake his head. This was a far more dangerous situation than anyone initially thought. Tucker Miles was beyond obsessed with Kassidy.

Now the hard part: what to tell Kassidy? There was no easy way to handle this. She'd been right the whole time. Someone had been in her house, and now they had the evidence to prove it. No comfort would come from her knowing what they had found. Sawyer contemplated: do you tell your victim in order to arm her with knowledge so she knows what she's dealing with? Or, do you keep her safe from this, knowing it would not only scare her and also scar her?

Scar, the image of Kassidy's legs impaled by the crudely built torture device flashed before his eyes. The urgency to find Tucker overwhelmed him. He tucked away the fear and dread of the thought of Tucker getting hold of Kassidy again and kept a straight face.

"I want everything photographed and logged into evidence!"

He thought of Kassidy's favorite saying: my God is stronger than his. He hoped she was right because with how this was headed, the outcome didn't look good for her. He didn't want to think about that right now. He had to keep his head clear.

"I think he's been living in this room," Officer Huffman uttered.

"What makes you think he wouldn't stay in his house that's only a couple blocks from hers? This church is on the other side of town?" Sawyer half turned toward Huffman.

"Because if I'm not mistaken you're standing on his bed."

Sawyer looked down and sure enough, there was a pillow off to the side and a couple of blankets on the floor. With a second glance, he realized these were also taken from Kassidy's home.

He had lost track of how many reports he had found where she'd called about missing items or items that had been moved around in her house. He owed her a huge apology. After seeing this room, no wonder she had been so adamant that someone had been in her house.

He guessed he and his team would need to cover why you can't get complacent on the job when you deal with someone from the public repeatedly. In Kassidy's case, she had been right all along, and he could see it in the officers' faces—they all thought the same thing.

No wonder, when Tucker had given them permission to search his house, he hadn't seemed too concerned. He had nothing to hide in his house. He had brought it all here: every precious item he had painstakingly stolen from Kassidy. This was his trophy room where he would no doubt lie for hours and stare at the walls before he fell asleep.

"Hey, Detective?" an officer hollered from the room as Sawyer turned to leave.

"Yes?"

Paper tore as the officer peeled sheets of it off the fourth wall. Small flakes of paint floated to the floor from the wall that at first appeared to be pristine and untouched by this lunatic. Echoes of paper being torn filled the room as more pieces were pulled free. They cleared away the paper to uncover what was underneath and a hush fell over them as the last piece of paper was removed.

The entire wall was painted with a hideous reddish-brown paint. It matched the color splashed on the pictures. Only on this wall, there were no pictures, only words. Scrawled in black choppy letters all over the wall were phrases written in every direction with several overlapping.

Kassidy is mine.

No, she isn't, she is to die.

Her soul will belong to my lord.

Leave her alone I made a mistake inviting you in.

Satan now owns you.

Then the most disturbing of them all: *She will never belong to you. My lord will destroy her.*

Sawyer leaned toward the wall to get a closer look at the paint. "Glove up guys, this isn't brown paint: it's blood."

The blood that had long since dried, made a blank canvas on which he wrote his disturbing thoughts. What bothered Sawyer was where did he get that much blood?

"Huffman make sure an officer's with Kassidy! I am going to the hospital! And tow his car to our evidence bay!" Sawyer sprinted down the hall as Kassidy filled his thoughts. This man would kill her and the urge Sawyer felt to protect her astounded him. He knew in that instant he'd die to keep her safe.

Sawyer sped to the hospital, lights and sirens all the way. His heart pounded thunderously in his chest. He'd dropped the ball on this one.

Why didn't he pull Tucker in for questioning? Maybe he could have scared him into talking. He should have trusted his gut on this. The creepy vibe he got from Tucker when he was in his house made his skin crawl. He had felt something was off with him, and how right he had been.

He had seen the fear in Kassidy's eyes when they were out at her house repeatedly; the frustration she expressed over the thought that none of them believed her; the absolute fear that someone stalked her. The worst was when someone had hacked off her hair while she slept. He had seen the guy in the house himself. Why didn't he run for the guy instead of toward Kassidy? Maybe he wouldn't have gotten away.

So many officers had written their reports as if it was just another mental health case; someone who wanted attention. He had always trusted his instincts before and they had never failed him. Some would say they had even saved his life a time or two.

There was nothing in her past to hint at any mental illness. In fact, she had absolutely nothing in her past—no history at all. Her childhood was void of any run-ins with police. She truly had one of those good girls next door, everyone's best friend pasts.

Sawyer was jaded, he knew he was. Everyone had something to hide. Something they had done at one time or another they were ashamed or embarrassed about. It was how the world was. Everyone always had a past. No one was that good and innocent in life. That's what first intrigued him about her. She was genuinely one of a kind. How did someone like her go from no worries in life to being stalked by the scariest individual he'd ever come across?

Officers cringed every time they were dispatched to her house. The mention of her address over the radio elicited groans throughout the station: 'What was it this time?' 'What did she do to set someone off?' 'Someone doesn't do something like this unless she set this in motion.' 'Did she lead this guy on?' 'Did she flirt with him first then give him the cold shoulder?'

Some officers even had a pool on whether she had done this to herself. Others had a pool on whether they would have a dozen roses logged into the evidence room by the time this was all done and over with. They had all seen it in the past, so they all asked the questions. Unfortunately, the fact was, ninety-nine percent of the time, something did start it.

Now, after he seeing Tucker's room there was more than enough evidence that Kassidy hadn't imagined any of it. He was overcome with the urge to get to her and protect her. He couldn't imagine her fear and all she'd been through today.

Sawyer knew he owed her a huge apology. How would he be able to keep her safe and locate Tucker at the same time? If the dates on some photos were correct, then he started watching her six months ago leading to his sick collection in his trophy room. Where else could he possibly hide? Was this the only room he had of her? Or were there more? Six months ago, he moved into his house. What did he do before he moved to New Kingdom? Were there other victims out there? Did he kill anyone?

He flipped the switch to turn off his lights and sirens about a block away from the hospital. Sawyer would feel much better once he was by Kassidy's side. He pulled into a parking space then sprinted toward the ER entrance. Relief flooded him as he saw another officer's SUV already in the parking lot.

At the nurse's station, he asked for Kassidy's room. The nurse pointed down the hall and advised him she was in bed seven.

He kept his eyes open for bed seven when he saw one of his officers camped outside the curtain. The officer waved Sawyer over and took a step toward him as he approached.

"How is she?" Sawyer couldn't hide the concern in his voice.

"A doctor's with her now, cleaning out her wounds. A few will need stitches. She had x-rays, and they said she's extremely lucky. It doesn't look like the nails hit anything major. It would do more damage to stitch the small ones than to just let her legs heal on their own. There are a couple that tore when she pulled herself off the board that needed stitches. The rest they will close with glue. The doctor said she'll be okay. She'll be sore for a few days but nothing that warrants his concern. Also, no fractures from the nails that hit the bone, but there's some bad bruising," Officer Johns answered. "So, is it really Tucker Miles?"

"Yes, and to think we were in his house and he seemed so normal. Almost too normal now that I think back. He's really messed up. He's going to kill her if we don't catch him." Sawyer's face flushed red as he thought about Kassidy kneeling on the board and the tears that had streamed down her face. He would never be able to get that image out of his head. He couldn't help but feel partial blame that she had to endure that mad man's torture. They hadn't found anything concrete until now. No fingerprints, no trace evidence left behind, nothing. Just like his house. It almost didn't look like anyone lived there. It almost looked like a sterile hospital environment.

"Too normal, Detective?" Officer John's eyes narrowed.

"Yeah, his house was spotlessly clean. No dishes in the sink. The daily newspaper laid out conveniently on the coffee table as if he read it while he drank his coffee. But now that I think back, he never had coffee in the coffee pot. It was clean and looked brand new. If you were going to drink a cup of coffee while reading the morning paper, would there still be coffee in your coffee pot? Or would you make one cup then take the time to clean the coffee maker before you read the paper? I wonder what else he's hiding since he was just heading out when we got there so we couldn't scrutinize his house too closely."

Sawyer knew he needed to see a judge to get a knock and talk for Tucker's house. He would also have the judge issue a warrant for Tucker for the felonious kidnapping and the assault on Kassidy. This time they'd go through his house with a fine-toothed comb.

"Did I hear right that there's a room in the church he was living in and it's all kinds of levels of messed up?" Officer Johns whispered.

"I've never seen anything like it in all my years on the force. He's been stalking her for months and has been in her house who knows how many times. More than I care to think about."

"So, she wasn't wrong about all those reports she filed?"

"No, not at all. He's probably been in her house at least a few hundred times and she only realized a few. He was just playing with her, and from the dates on the pictures, this started well over six months ago."

"Six months!"

"Shh, keep your voice down, Officer, we aren't sure how we'll tell Kassidy. I don't want her any more upset or stressed out than she has been." Sawyer's voice had more of an edge to it than he planned.

"Tell me about what?" The doctor pulled the curtain back with the scrape of metal rings along the bar just as the nurse wheeled Kassidy out of the exam room. They'd wrapped her legs like a mummy and there were a couple of spots where the blood gave away where her punctures were.

"She's ready to go home. She'll need to fill these prescriptions for pain meds and antibiotics. Her legs will ache after the injections we gave her wears off." The doctor handed Sawyer two prescription slips to take to the pharmacy.

"We'll make sure to get these filled." Sawyer turned to Kassidy and handed her the prescriptions and smiled. "I'll take you home if you could hold onto those for me?"

"Okay. Now, tell me about what?" Kassidy tentatively asked.

"Let's get these filled then get you home. We'll sit down and discuss what we've found then go over our options. Does that sound okay to you?" Sawyer dreaded the upcoming conversation he was about to have with Kassidy.

"Yes, on one condition. You tell me everything and leave nothing out." Kassidy's eyes met his.

"Deal. Now let's get you out of here." Sawyer bent down and half whispered. "I don't like hospitals, just so you know."

After he wheeled her to his car, Sawyer opened the passenger door to help her sit down. She winced as her skin strained against the stitches. He took the wheelchair back to the entrance where a nurse relieved him of it. Sawyer didn't say anything on the drive to the pharmacy, afraid he wouldn't stop after he started. He didn't want to have this conversation in the car.

After they filled her prescriptions, it was a dull drive to her house. Sawyer expertly drove as if on cruise control. If he'd only listened to his instincts before now. He'd been here more times than he should have.

"I don't see any police cars." Kassidy looked around.

"No, you won't. They parked down the street and came in on foot. Just in case he came back to the house after he got away from us at the church."

"Okay, you need to talk." Kassidy trembled.

"Stay in the car and lock the doors until I come out and get you."

"Detective Riggs!"

"Please, just give me one minute to check on the officers then we'll talk, I promise." He gently placed his hand on hers. She tensed for a split second before she relaxed again.

FOR THE FIRST TIME, Kassidy saw Sawyer as more than just the detective handling her case.

He crept up the stairs as he drew his gun then peeked around the door into the house. He opened the screen door then stepped in, calling out to the officers as he entered.

Kassidy sat uneasily in the car. She looked every which way as if peering eyes watched her. She was no longer safe in her neighborhood. An image flashed across her mind of her door flying in as the frame splintered into her bedroom. It made her shudder. Now as she thought back, every noise in her house was an ominous omen that he was there. Sawyer had told her to get a gun for her own protection. She wasn't sure she could own a gun. The thought of taking a life made her sick to her stomach. No, a gun wasn't for her; maybe a large breed dog. She kicked herself for getting those stupid shrieking alarms instead of a dog. She'd go to the local shelter tomorrow. A dog would be something new and exciting to her. She'd never had one before, but she always loved her friends' dogs. Thoughts of the shelter were on her mind when the back door opened and Sawyer started down the steps.

The other two officers exited her house before Sawyer reached the car door and waved as they headed down the street toward their patrol cars. On their way, she noticed they pointed to different areas around the neighborhood and chatted about what they motioned to.

Kassidy took the steps one at a time and winced as her skin tugged at the stitches and glue on her legs

"You need to sit down. I can make you tea." Sawyer took the kettle from Kassidy.

"You promised you would tell me everything." Kassidy limped to a stool at the island in her kitchen. Sawyer moved another stool so it faced her then raised her legs to rest on it.

"Yes, I did." Sawyer raised his hands as if to ask where everything was. Kassidy told him where the cups, tea, and sugar were.

"I also take milk in mine" She added.

"Wow, you like your tea wimpy, don't you?" Sawyer tried to break the ice.

"Don't change the subject, please. Just tell me. I know it's bad. How much worse can it get? Have you not seen my legs?" Her voice broke.

"We know it's Tucker. He's been in and out of your house for the last six months." Sawyer turned from Kassidy. He pulled the tea, sugar, and a cup out of the cabinet, then placed the milk on the counter.

"Six months?" Her voice came out in a whisper as the reality of that sunk in. It chilled her to her soul.

"Yes, we found a, um, room at the church. It shows he's probably been watching you since he moved to town."

"But I never even talked to him. Why would he do this?" Kassidy rested her head in her hands.

"We don't know but it looks like he's been coming in here for at least six months. We found a trophy room. As far as we can tell, everything he has taken from here is in that room. The room was in the basement of the church he took you to. Including but not limited to your toothbrush and hair." Sawyer diverted his eyes as he said the last.

He brought her the cup, tea, sugar, and milk. Then asked where the spoons were. She pointed to the drawer.

Kassidy wanted this to be over. She took the spoon from Sawyer and their fingers met. Each held onto a part of the spoon for a split second longer, then Sawyer let go. Tears pooled in her eyes until one made it over the edge of her lower eyelid and cascaded down her cheek as the rest followed.

"Miss Parker, I'm sorry. I didn't want to tell you everything because I didn't want to scare you any more than you already have been. However, I also wanted you to know what we're dealing with and how messed up this guy is. You have to know what he's capable of."

Milk swirled in her tea. The swirl disappeared as she added a spoon of sugar and began to stir.

"We'll continue to have someone outside your house twenty-four hours a day and we'll add another officer at the front of the house."

"No offense, but he took me out of this house with an officer outside. Who's to say he can't do it again but next time he kills me?" Kassidy shook.

"I want to add an officer in the house if you will let me, so you are never alone in here."

"I don't know. I just don't know." She took a sip of her tea and closed her eyes as more tears broke free and trailed down her cheeks. She swung her legs off the stool and winced. Her skin was stiff and unmoving against the stitches and glue.

"Where are your prescriptions? They gave you one for pain and said you'd start to feel it soon." Sawyer's eyes scanned the kitchen counters but didn't see them.

"I might have left them in the car."

"I'll be right back." Sawyer bounded down the steps to the car to retrieve her prescriptions.

Eighteen

SAWYER'S HEART DROPPED when he came back into the kitchen and saw that Kassidy wasn't there. Instinct caused his hand to go to the grip of his Glock as he pushed the two-point locking mechanism, freeing his gun. His eyes, from years of working in law enforcement, scrutinized the room. Her tea on the counter. The stool still pulled away from the island. He listened and slowed his breathing. Then he heard her voice down the hall.

"Miss Parker?" Sawyer called out as he started down the hall, his heartbeat quickened. He jogged into the bedroom, his gun half drawn out of the holster until he saw her. Kassidy's face was pale. He holstered his gun as she stood motionless with the phone up to her ear.

He gently took the phone. "Who's this?"

"Oh, isn't it Mr. Hero Detective Riggs!"

"Tucker, just turn yourself in. Don't make it harder on you than it already is." Sawyer's voice was soothing as he tried to calmly talk to Tucker who yelled on the other end of the phone.

"You don't get to keep her; she's mine!" His voice slithered through the phone

"What makes you say that, Tucker?" Sawyer yanked his cell phone out of his pocket. With a quick call to the station, he told dispatch to try and trace the call from Tucker.

"Sorry sir, he has it blocked. We can't trace it," dispatch informed him.

Sawyer snapped his phone shut then jammed it into his pocket.

"I saw her first. You never even knew about her until I acted." Tucker sounded as if he'd called dibs on her. It made Sawyer's skin crawl.

Tucker hung up, so Sawyer handed her phone back. "Is there a way to block all calls that come in unavailable to your phone?"

"I'm not sure, but wouldn't that anger him more?"

"Probably, but it could also force him out into the open and then we can catch him."

"My God is stronger than his."

"I've heard you say that before. What do you mean by that?"

"Do you mind if we sit down? My legs are killing me." Kassidy limped past him, down the hall to get her tea and her pain meds.

Sawyer followed her as she crossed into the living room and sat in a chair with an ottoman in front. He helped her lift her legs onto the ottoman before he sat on the couch.

"What do you believe? In terms of faith, I mean. If you don't mind me asking?" Kassidy was forward with her question but not in a rude, abrupt way.

"I never really went to church as a kid and now as an adult, it never crossed my mind to go. Figure since I didn't go as a kid, I don't need to go now." Sawyer was brutally honest.

"Well, I grew up in a church. Went to one all my life. I thank my parents for that. They helped save my soul from hell." She smiled.

"Hell?" Sawyer wasn't sure he wanted to get into this conversation but he also didn't want to leave her alone. Maybe it would explain why she said that phrase. If he could glean some insight into Kassidy, maybe it would help them figure out what drew Tucker to her. Then they could catch him.

"In the Bible, it explains that God sent His son to die for our sins. That everyone is born a sinner. No one is good enough to get to Heaven on their own. Not through good deeds or being a good person. Nothing washes away that sin; it's too great. Except for Jesus Christ. He came to earth and died for us—for you and for me. What we have to do is simple: accept that He died for us and that we're sinners and live our life for Him. Ask Him to come into our hearts and ask for forgiveness for our sins. He'll wash you clean. That's the only way to Heaven. The world's proof that Satan exists. Look at all the horrible things that are happening. Did you see Tucker today?"

"Well, of course, I did. What do you mean?"

"Did you see the black in his eyes?"

"Yes, he has dark-colored eyes." Sawyer shrugged.

"You realize he was possessed by a demon and that demon controlled him?"

"Possessed? That doesn't happen in real life, Miss Parker." Sawyer felt she was very fragile after the past couple of weeks and he didn't want to upset her.

"Please call me Kassidy, and yes it does. Didn't you hear the difference in his voice? That his eyes were a light color when his voice wasn't dark and creepy?"

"It was just the lighting in the abandoned church and with nothing in the sanctuary, it's bound to distort his voice. He played off of that to scare you." He hoped he made sense.

"When you become a born-again Christian, it's impossible for a demon to take possession of you. The Holy Spirit lives in your heart and is so powerful because it's a part of God that nothing can overpower. Hence the statement we say in our church, 'My God is stronger than yours.' It's true; no one's stronger than He is. Have you ever read the Bible?"

He felt as if she was looking right into him. "No, I never had a Bible."

"Open that drawer on the end table next to you. Take that one." Kassidy offered.

"Oh no, I couldn't take your Bible. I really don't think it's for me. No offense." Sawyer balked at the thought of carrying a Bible.

Kassidy laughed. "It's not my only one."

"You have more than one?"

"Yes, I have several. Please take it. Read it with an open mind. It will shock you at God's love for His people. He gave Israel so many chances and kept giving them chances because He doesn't want anyone to be lost. But He also gives us free will. Which is why Tucker's the way he is. He invited that demon in because it promised to help him get me." Kassidy trembled at the last statement.

Sawyer had the drawer open but didn't pick up the Bible right away. There was a weight to it. He couldn't explain why, since the actual weight of the Bible shouldn't make it feel this heavy. He'd never held a Bible before and it made him nervous. He wasn't sure why. It was just a book.

"It's okay. It won't hurt you. It'll change you in ways you can't imagine." Kassidy smiled, one of the first real smiles he'd seen since meeting her. He had to say it looked good on her. She was beautiful. But there was something else in that smile; something pure; something he couldn't put his finger on but it shone in her eyes.

"Okay, I'll borrow this, but I can't promise anything." Sawyer smiled back at her.

Kassidy had finished her tea, "Detective Riggs?"

Sawyer jumped up. "Miss Parker?" As he squatted beside her, he tilted up her drooping head.

"Something's wrong. I don't feel right." Fear clouded her face. He hoped it wasn't a reaction to one of the medications?

"Come on, let's get up and walk around. Are you allergic to anything that could have been in the prescriptions?" Sawyer grabbed his phone out of his pocket. He dialed the station and demanded an ambulance.

The back door opened as an officer rushed in, gun drawn. "Sir, what's going on?"

"I don't know if she has an allergy to one of her prescriptions or if it's something else. Take samples to the lab of the tea, sugar, and milk on the counter, just to make sure." Sawyer motioned with his arm where to look. He noticed the sugar was gone. He snatched his gun out of his holster and turned a full 360 in the kitchen. The officer did the same, alerted to the Detective's movements.

"He was in here. The sugar's gone. He put something in the sugar!"

The officer called for backup on his radio, then stood with his back to Sawyer. They watched for anything that would alert them that Tucker was still in the house.

"Miss Parker. Kassidy, stay awake for me. Come on, stay awake." Sawyer struggled to hold her up. Her head lolled to the side and she took in shallow breaths.

The ambulance pulled up outside and Henry and Josh jumped out. With their first-in-kits slung over their shoulders they sprinted for the door.

"Henry there was something in the sugar. She had a cup of tea when I brought her home from the hospital." Sawyer exclaimed, holstering his weapon.

Henry grabbed her wrist to check her pulse. "Pulse is slow and with her breathing, my guess would be an opioid overdose. But which one? Did she take her prescription when she got home? If he put something in the sugar, the dose of the prescription could have been too much.

Josh, grab me the Narcan. That will help until we get her loaded up and transported." Henry frowned as he gently pushed on her blue nailbeds.

Henry peeled back the package, removed the Narcan device, then tried to administer it when she started to fight back. Sawyer wrapped his arms around her waist and tried to control her arms. Josh also grabbed her arms to keep her from pushing them away as Henry tried to follow her head, which she turned toward Sawyer's chest.

"Come on, Kass, you have to do this for a moment. I know it's not fun but we have to." Henry put one hand on her forehead and held it in place as Sawyer held her chin. Between the three of them, they finally got her restrained enough to administer the Narcan. She started to come around fully now and didn't fight them as much.

"Josh, grab the O2, and let's get that on her." Henry took away the Narcan as Kassidy opened her eyes. "Hey, there she is."

With the oxygen mask over her nose and mouth, Kassidy took in large gulps of air.

"What happened to keeping him out of her house?" Henry snapped at Sawyer.

"Hey, I was right here. I don't know how he got in. I think we need to look at this house and see what we missed. How's she doing?" Sawyer shook with anger. Tucker could have killed her.

"She's coming around but I want to get her transported as soon as possible." Henry nodded toward Josh. "Grab the stretcher."

"No, I can walk," Kassidy argued.

"Wow, she's stubborn." Sawyer held her close.

"Oh, you have no idea," Henry added.

Sawyer and Henry each took a side to help walk her out to the waiting ambulance.

"Do you really think I need to go? I'm doing better." Kassidy dreaded another trip to the hospital.

"Oh, you're not arguing with me on this. Narcan is temporary. We have to transport you, so the hospital can clear out the drugs in your system. Plus, Celeste would kill me if I didn't get you checked out."

"Then Sawyer can drive me. No offense but I don't want to ride in an ambulance again anytime soon."

Henry persisted. "What if something happens on the way that you need medical attention? I'm sorry, Kass. Policy on any overdose where we have treated with Narcan—we have to transport."

Two more police cars pulled up as Sawyer and Henry got her to the back of the ambulance but she refused to budge. She couldn't imagine being in the back of an ambulance yet again.

"Sorry, I agree with Henry. You have to go by ambulance. I won't take you." Sawyer didn't move.

Josh unloaded the stretcher, undid the straps and then patiently waited for Henry and Sawyer.

Kassidy started to feel dizzy again and started to take slow breaths as if she couldn't pull in enough air.

Henry put the oxygen mask back on. "See, this is why we have to transport you."

Sawyer and Henry helped her up onto the stretcher. She leaned back and closed her eyes. Josh buckled the straps then loaded her into the back of the ambulance.

"I'll meet you over there," Sawyer snapped, louder than he meant to.

Henry climbed into the back of the ambulance and Sawyer saw him glance in his direction. He attempted to smile. Not many people saw his anger and he was mad at himself for letting it show in front of Henry. Sawyer closed the back doors on the ambulance and gave a good thump on them letting Josh know, who had gotten behind the wheel, that they were secure. He jumped into his unmarked unit and gunned the engine.

Sawyer closely followed the ambulance. He wasn't letting them out of his sight. They made their way to the hospital on the other side of town.

Sawyer walked into the hospital after finding a place to park. The parking lot was busier than normal. Henry motioned him over.

"What have they found?"

"It's what I thought: opioid overdoes. Mix it in with sugar and you can't taste it. They're going to keep her for observation. It doesn't look like she got very much into her system for a relapse. What kind of sick person would do that to someone else?"

"Trust me you don't want to know how sick he is. You wouldn't sleep at night." Images of the room in the church flashed through Sawyer's mind.

"So, what're you going to do to keep her safe until you guys can catch him?"

"I have my best officers going through every inch of her house to see how he's getting in. If we can at least stop him there, he'll have to come out in the open to get to her. Then we can catch him." Sawyer paced.

"Well, she'll stay with me and Celeste until you catch him."

"No. With what he's done already, I couldn't live with myself if he did something to you or Celeste because I was at your house." Kassidy called out from behind the curtain that provided privacy around her ER bed.

"We're keeping her overnight. We'll see how she is in the morning to determine if we'll release her tomorrow. She's determined to go home but we refuse to release her tonight." The doctor turned toward the nurses' station to see who his next patient was.

"What do you mean you won't stay with me and Celeste? We'll be fine. I don't see him coming in the house with three of us there." Henry stated as he walked to the end of her gurney.

"In her defense, he came in the house with me there and an officer outside. If the police weren't enough to scare him, he won't hesitate to come in with just you three there."

"Then how do you keep her safe? Who knows what else he could've put in her food at her house?" Henry threw his hands up in the air.

"I'll take her to the store tomorrow and get her new groceries for just a couple days then throw out everything in her house." Sawyer gave Kassidy a stern look.

"Okay, why take the sugar bowl? If he put it in other food, why not leave the sugar bowl, so it guaranteed I would use it." Kassidy met his stare.

"We're not taking the chance."

Henry waved as he and Josh pushed the stretcher out to the ambulance and got ready for their next call.

Sawyer helped Kassidy into a waiting wheelchair that the nurse had rolled into her ER room a few moments before. "We'll figure something out. All fresh produce and items in your fridge I say are off limits. We can discuss the frozen items later."

The nurse took her to the elevator. Pushed the up arrow, and waited for the elevator to take them to the room Kassidy would sleep in for the night while they monitored her.

Sawyer stalked out of the emergency room toward his car. He wanted to get the report typed tonight while his mind raced in several different directions.

Nineteen

SAWYER WAS AT THE HOSPITAL bright and early the next morning. He tapped his foot as he rode the elevator up to the third floor where they informed him Kassidy's room was. As he got off the elevator, he strolled up to the nurse's station to ask for her specific room number. He knocked softly on the door. She answered that he could come in. As he tiptoed into the room, he wasn't surprised to see her perched on the edge of her bed, dressed and ready to leave.

"Grocery store first?" Sawyer prodded.

"I need to go home and get my purse. I would say anything frozen and in its original package is okay right?" She cringed as she pictured all the food she had stored in her house.

"I say it depends on what it is and if there are any puncture marks in the package."

"Well, we can look when we get back to the house, then I'll know what I need to replace when I get to the store." Sawyer didn't look at Kassidy as she said it. He would need to reason with her when they got to her house about the possibility of all her food being tainted, not just the sugar.

They pulled up to her driveway several moments later. It was a quiet drive to her house. Neither one said a word. He saw the fear in her face as she looked at the numerous police cars crowding the street behind her house. Two officers anxiously approached Sawyer's side of the car. Sawyer talked in hushed tones with the two officers.

"Show me." He walked with the two officers, then pointed to another officer and yelled. "Don't leave her side!"

An officer walked up and stood a couple of steps from her with a no-nonsense look on his face. The aviator sunglasses that hid part of his face concealed any emotions.

"What's going on?" Kassidy kept an eye on the back door where Sawyer and the other two officers disappeared.

"Ma'am, I'll let the Detective tell you." He didn't smile when she looked up at him.

Kassidy took a step toward her house when he put his arm out to block her way. "Please, just wait for the Detective."

"But it's my house and I want to know what's going on."

Sawyer stepped out into the sun and motioned for the officer to bring Kassidy up.

"What's going on?" Kassidy's voice broke as she climbed the stairs.

"We know how he's been getting in your house." His furrowed brow matched his frown.

"How?"

"Come on, I'll show you." Sawyer took a step back then headed down the hallway to her bedroom. Once in her walk-in closet, he pointed up to the attic access.

"How can he get in from up there? There's no way to get into the attic beside this." Kassidy placed her hand on a rung of the ladder propped against the open attic hatch.

"Go ahead, I'm right behind you." Sawyer nodded.

She took a step toward the ladder, winced, and looked at Sawyer. He nodded. She took a step up and then looked at him, eye level. He only nodded and smiled, to assure her he was right behind her.

She clambered into the attic and took Officer Huffman's hand as she made it to the top of the ladder. Sawyer was right behind her like he'd promised and she looked around her storage area, not sure what she was supposed to see. Her Christmas decorations and storage tubs were all where they normally were. She shrugged her shoulders to Sawyer.

"This way." Sawyer stepped around her and walked past the tubs to an area hidden out of sight from the entrance into the attic.

There, lurking behind the towers of storage tubs, were boards laid out as if to make a floor. There was a sleeping bag, pillow, and a blowup chair, along with several other items that hinted someone had been living in her attic.

Sawyer watched Kassidy's color drain from her face. She made it a few staggering steps.

"Miss Parker?" Sawyer stepped up to her as Huffman caught her when her legs crumpled from underneath her

Huffman easily picked her up, and turned toward the ladder, "I'll take her downstairs."

Sawyer climbed down first. Huffman lowered her into Sawyer's waiting arms. He gently carried her over to the bed and laid her down.

Huffman walked up behind Sawyer and grimaced at her lifeless form. "Sir, I'm not sure she'll get over this. This guy is even creeping me out."

"Make sure you guys bag everything up there."

"Everything? Ya know he's been relieving himself up there, don't ya?" Huffman raised his eyebrows.

"We can have biohazard come clean that up and dispose of it. Everything else I want in evidence. He's somewhere, but not up there. So, let's make sure there isn't any other room he's living in and make sure this house is secure. Maybe she can get some sleep since we know how he's been moving things around in the house without setting off the alarms. He didn't have to use the doors. He was already inside."

"The rest of the house is secure. After I saw that upstairs, I double-checked every possible way in myself. There ain't no way he can get back in this house." Huffman wasn't someone you wanted to tangle with.

"I'm never sleeping again." Kassidy slowly sat up. "Did I faint?"

"Yeah, you did," Huffman stated, then left the room. A couple of minutes later he had returned with evidence bags, as she raised her head out of her hands.

"Oh, my gosh. I'm so embarrassed. I've never fainted before." Kassidy still had no color in her face.

"Don't be; I didn't like seeing that either. But hey, at least we now know how he was in here. He's more than likely been in here living in your attic off and on the entire time."

"THAT DOESN'T MAKE ME feel better in the least bit." Kassidy hobbled down to the kitchen with her tea kettle in hand. She filled it with water then set it on the stove.

"No way. We haven't replaced your food yet. I won't let you make tea with what happened earlier." Sawyer had one hand on his gun holster and the other on his opposite hip in that famous cop stance she swore they taught in the police academy.

"Look." Kassidy stepped over to her pantry and pointed to the top row in the back. There were several unopened bags of sugar.

He raised a single eyebrow but reached up and took down a bag. As they stood in the pantry light, he pulled his flashlight and examined every square inch of the bag to look for any puncture hole or sign someone had tampered with it. Hesitantly he handed her the bag.

"See, this is a new bag and no signs it's been messed with. I think since he only took the sugar maybe that was all he put the drugs into." Kassidy wasn't sure who she was trying to convince more—Sawyer or herself.

"Well, I still say it's a bad idea. You don't go anywhere without an officer with you to make sure. Do you hear me?"

"I ask for one exception," Kassidy smirked. "Not when I'm in the bathroom."

Sawyer roared with laughter. "Deal."

An officer strolled in, handed Sawyer a tablet then strolled back to his post. It was the same officer that had kept Kassidy from entering her house earlier.

"What fitness tracker do you have?" Sawyer turned on the tablet then selected the app list for fitness trackers.

Kassidy held up her wrist for him to get a look at it. "It's an off-brand, but it does great. I haven't had any issues with it tracking my runs."

Sawyer gripped her wrist to get a look at the name, he saw the goosebumps appear on her arm then let go of her wrist. He typed in the name of her fitness tracker. With the app downloading, he glanced at Kassidy. A grin pulled at the corners of her mouth as she watched him expertly select everything.

"What?" Sawyer stared at her.

"Well, I'm shocked."

"Why?"

"Well, with the phone you have, I wasn't sure you knew what a tablet was, much less how to use one." Kassidy turned her back as she smiled and grabbed a cup out of the cabinet.

Huffman scoffed from the doorway as his enormous hands gripped several evidence bags from the attic.

"Oh, don't you start. I know how to use electronics. I just don't like the huge smartphones that are out there. A phone is a phone. I don't need all of this on my phone." He gestured at the tablet.

Huffman chuckled as he continued through the kitchen, then out the back door. He lugged all the bags down to his car, where he loaded them into the trunk.

"Why are you downloading my fitness tracker?" Kassidy pulled the singing tea kettle off the stove. As she reached the spoon toward the sugar, her heartbeat skipped. Her lips moved as she prayed that he hadn't touched this bag of sugar; then she added a heaping spoon to her tea.

"Because, if he takes you again, I can track you and get to you without him knowing it. I hope he won't think of that and make you take it off." Sawyer tapped a few times on the screen and connected it with the Bluetooth to her tracker. She felt it vibrate which confirmed it had linked to his tablet. She was glad she got the GPS tracking option.

"Did you want anything?" Kassidy held up her tea.

"Water would be great."

Kassidy opened the refrigerator, selected a bottle of water then handed it to Sawyer. She picked up her tea and proceeded to the front room.

"Thanks." He trailed her.

"So, since you've found his little hide-out in my attic, does this mean he can't get back in here since he isn't here now?" Kassidy didn't even want to think about what he'd watched her do in her house. She shuddered about all the times she'd showered.

"That's what we hope."

"So, what do we do now?"

"HOPEFULLY WE CAN GET him out in the open and arrest him then he should go away for a long time since we have him on felonious kidnapping with first-degree assault. The seriousness of what he's done should get him sent away for good. But you never know what a lawyer may put on the table as a deal for him." Sawyer hoped the guy couldn't afford a good lawyer and would have to settle for court-appointed defense. He wasn't saying court-appointed was bad, but he also saw what pricey lawyers could do to twist everything to their agenda.

Huffman made a third trip to the car with evidence bags then walked back into the house. He propped himself against the doorframe of the living room. "That's all of it. Biohazard will come to headquarters tomorrow to dispose of the waste which was loaded into the detention van. No one wanted it in their car. Then they'll clean the detention van."

"Sounds good. We'll keep two officers posted at her house, one on the front and one on the back hopefully to deter him from wanting to come back to pay Miss Parker a visit." Sawyer stood and walked Huffman out to the car and stopped to speak with the officer at the back door. He sauntered back into the house and lingered in the doorway of the living room.

"We're leaving. Keep my number close. I have the GPS on your tracker. Maybe just stay in for the afternoon. I'll have officers outside your house all night. If you hear anything you run to them. Do you hear me?"

"Yes." Kassidy got to her feet and followed him to the back door. "Detective Riggs, thank you for everything you've done. I appreciate it more than you know. I'm sorry I accused you of being involved."

"No need to apologize. I wouldn't know what to think either if I were in the same situation. But apology accepted." Sawyer winked at her before he turned around and left.

Twenty

A QUICK TRIP TO THE store and Kassidy was back home a short time later. All the minor essentials needed for her every day guilty pleasures, such as her tea, were put away. The old was either poured down the sink or discarded into her trashcan.

Kassidy dawdled in her kitchen. Her house was eerily quiet. That used to be the one thing she loved about her house more than anything—the peace and quiet it gave her. No! She decided this was still her house and a good home-cooked meal and movie were in order for the night. The lock had a mind of its own and after a couple fights with it, she opened the back door to the officer who stood outside.

"Did you guys want dinner? I'm getting ready to make some and it would be no big deal to make enough for everyone here," she beamed.

"No thanks, ma'am. Officer Huffman's bringing us dinner." The officer was all business and turned back toward his post then half turned back. "Thanks for the offer though, we appreciate it."

Kassidy went to the freezer and picked a choice pork chop she had bought in bulk and had vacuum-sealed with the marinade in individual portions for herself. She also chose an ear of corn. She walked to the cabinet then pulled out a box of long grain rice. Happy with the choice for dinner, she turned on the indoor grill.

Kassidy made short work of cooking her dinner. With her TV turned on, the starting credits rolled over the screen with the theme music announcing the start of the movie. She laid out her meal on a table slid over in front of her favorite chair. Dinner and a movie were great. It helped her to relax knowing Tucker wasn't in her house.

Her phone rang, so she jumped up to answer it. It said Celeste on the caller ID but that tended to be wrong. She hesitantly answered. "Hello?"

"Hey Kass, what are you doing for dinner?" It *was* Celeste.

"I ate, sorry." Kassidy smiled. It felt good to feel almost normal in her house. She grabbed the dishes from the living room and took them to the kitchen to put in the dishwasher.

"Please don't tell me you ate the food at your place after what Henry told me?" Celeste's voice became high pitched as she finished her question.

"Celeste, calm down, we think he only laced my sugar. He took that to hide the evidence. I grabbed some things from the store today and inspected the food from my freezer carefully before I cooked it. I even made sure the packaging was intact," Kassidy slowly relayed to her friend.

"Kass, how can you even take that chance?"

"Celeste, would God let something happen if it wasn't in His plan? Come on, you know if you put it in God's hands, He will always take care of you." Kassidy loaded the dishwasher then ambled down the hall to her bedroom. Her legs screamed. The prescription pain meds made her head swim and feel as if her entire body was numb. Prescription pain meds were not for her and she would not finish the bottle that she had.

She stopped dead at the doorway to her bedroom; she found she didn't want to cross the threshold into her room. "Hello, earth to Kass. Are You Listening?" Celeste still talked but Kassidy didn't hear it.

"I'm sorry, Celeste, I think I may sleep in the spare bedroom tonight instead of my room." Kassidy turned on all the lights.

"Why would you do that?"

Oh right. Her and Henry didn't know about what the officers found in the attic. She casually told Celeste everything the officers discovered. Celeste was beside herself and yelled for Henry in her high-pitched frantic voice. Kassidy pictured her friend animated as she explained it all to her husband.

"You are staying here until they catch him. Henry's coming over to get you right now. Pack a bag; you're coming here and no arguing."

"No, I'm staying here. I decided he isn't chasing me out of my house. Maybe if I show I'm not scared of him, he'll lose interest in trying to get me." Kassidy was proud of herself for realizing this was what she wanted to do.

"You can't be serious!"

"I am serious. Who better to watch over me than God? You know our motto and it's true," Kassidy grabbed a pair of pajamas and shuffled to the spare bedroom to settle in for the night. It was weird not being in her own room, but hey, one bed was just as good as another.

"Henry, talk to her."

Kassidy smiled, "Hello, Henry."

"Hey, Kass." Henry didn't say anything. No one talked Kassidy out of something once her mind was made up.

"So, I'm going to bed now. I'll talk to you two in the morning." Kassidy giggled at what the conversation would be like at Celeste and Henry's house.

It surprised her how comfortable the bed was. No one had ever slept in it. The bed conformed to her and seemed to pull her into the soft pillow top of the mattress. She never even felt herself fall asleep.

She awoke with a start. Frozen in place, she didn't move but just listened. Ding Dong. It was her doorbell. She jumped up, grabbed her robe off the end of the bed and tied it around her waist. She jogged down to the kitchen then limped up to the back door. The brightness of the sun shocked her as she squinted at the dark shadow of a man in her doorway. How was it so bright outside already?

Sawyer stood there with concern on his face as her eyes adjusted to the brightness.

"What? What happened?" Kassidy was now fully awake.

"You didn't answer your phone and your friend Celeste called the police department when you didn't answer her text messages this morning." Sawyer stepped up a step and peered into the house.

Kassidy stepped to the side and looked for the clock on the stove. "What time is it?"

"It's seven thirty-five." Sawyer filled the doorway of the kitchen.

"What? I haven't slept that late in years."

Sawyer narrowed his eyes at her. "Do you feel sluggish or anything to suggest the food you cooked yesterday had anything in it?"

"Oh no, not at all. I think lack of sleep finally caught up with me. I feel great. Better than I have in a long time." Kassidy looked up at his hulking form that blocked out most of the sun from the doorway.

Sawyer's shoulders relaxed. "You better call Celeste. I think her and Henry are on their way over here."

She expertly scrolled through her phone numbers and dialed Celeste's phone.

"Kassidy!" Celeste squealed into the phone.

"Oh my gosh! Calm down; I was sleeping." Kassidy grinned at Sawyer who stepped back down the steps as he closed the door behind him.

"You have never not answered your phone. How dare you scare me like that?" Celeste scolded as her voice finally dropped to an octave that didn't want to shatter eardrums.

"I'm fine. I had a fantastic night's sleep is all." Kassidy limped a little as she walked down the hallway to her room. The pain meds had completely worn off. With her phone balanced on her shoulder by her cheek, she managed to change into her running gear. As Celeste's rant continued, Kassidy sat the phone on the dresser while she put her hair into a ponytail. She snatched the phone off the dresser and took long strides down the hall to the kitchen, trying to stretch her legs. With a fresh bottle of water, she downed antibiotics and acetaminophen.

"Well, you scared me and Henry half to death. We still think you need to stay with us until this is all over."

"I liked sleeping in my house last night. I had one of the best nights of sleep in a long time. I'm going for a run. I'll talk to you later."

"What? Are you inviting him to grab you again? You can't run with your legs the way they are either!" Celeste screeched through the phone so that Kassidy had to pull the phone away from her ear.

"Calm down, Celeste, Detective Riggs linked an app on his tablet so he can see where I am through my fitness tracker. I'll have him keep an eye on it to make sure I only stay on the route I want to go today. Goodbye, Celeste, I have to get going. I promise I'll be okay and I'll call you when I get back." Kassidy grabbed her armband for her phone and her earbuds.

With the back door open, she saw Sawyer loitering by his vehicle. She waved at him, after she locked her back door, to let him know she'd be down to talk to him. He stepped away from the officer and met her halfway down the driveway.

"I'm going for a run if you want to test your app to make sure it tracks correctly." Kassidy looked up at him. Sunglasses slid over her eyes blocked the intensity of the morning sun.

"Do you think it's a good idea? Won't the glue open back up?" Sawyer tilted his head eyeing her legs.

"I'll be fine. I took acetaminophen and antibiotics, plus we have to check out the app anyway. I'll let you know where I'm going so you can make sure if I venture off that route you need to look for me. I'll go at a much slower pace than I normally do and may only do one or two miles depending on how the legs feel."

"Okay, where are you going?" He asked as he headed back to his car and reached in to grab the tablet off the passenger seat.

Kassidy took a couple of minutes to let him know the route she'd found on her mapping system. It would still let her get her full five miles in, hopefully. Sawyer wrote it down then looked down at her as she took off. She put her earbuds in as her songs played and filled her head with music.

She found a good stride but had to keep it slower than her normal running pace. It felt good to be out of her house and back on the road. Her legs were tender, but she hoped to work through it. She smiled as she turned up her music just a bit more. Still able to hear outside noises, her face relaxed as she made her first turn.

There was comfort in knowing it was Tucker Miles. She didn't hesitate to wave at those she passed. She would call Detective Riggs if she even thought she saw a glimpse of Tucker. Her legs burned as she turned down the next street and a quick release of taught skin made her think she popped a stitch. Still, she pushed on. She was excited at the different scenery and took it all in as she ran. Maybe she had been in a rut.

For the first time in weeks, she started to feel like herself again. A smile spread across her face. She couldn't help but feel as if the Lord was with her as she ran. She picked up speed and saw the next street she needed to turn onto in the distance.

She made the next turn and thought about what she would do today. With it being such a beautiful day, she thought maybe open all the windows of her house and deep clean some areas she didn't clean all the time, such as behind the fridge and under the stove. Maybe even move the couches and vacuum under those as well.

Before she knew it, she was already on the next street. On the final stretch of road that would take her back to her house, she slowed down as another pop in her skin worried her. With the sun fully up she sweated more than usual and she reminded herself if she slept this late again to bring a small towel to wipe her face with, to keep the sweat out of her eyes.

Her house was in the distance and she could just make out the officers' car. Detective Riggs sat on the hood of his car with the tablet in his hands. The officer also watched the tablet. There was comfort in knowing that Detective Riggs knew where she was.

Detective Riggs looked in her direction. That could only mean he knew she wasn't far from the house, and he waved. She waved back and kept her steady pace until she got closer to the driveway. Now slowed down to a normal walk she stepped into her driveway and started up her back stairs as Detective Riggs put the tablet back in the car.

"How was the run? You had a good pace going."

"Thanks, it was great to be out there again. I had to keep it slower than I normally do. Everything good inside?" Kassidy wouldn't be using the master bedroom shower quite yet.

"All quiet. I can go through it if you prefer." Sawyer motioned to the officer who took the key from Kassidy, proceeded up the stairs then let himself in through the back door.

Sawyer followed him with his gun out and disappeared around the corner. Several agonizing seconds ticked by as she shifted from one foot to the other, when both re-emerged from the confines of her house.

"Good to go." Sawyer holstered his gun.

"Thanks." Kassidy took the key from the officer then locked the door behind her after she stepped into her kitchen. A scalding hot shower made her feel like a new person. The cuts that had split open on her run stung as the hot water hit them. The water turned a pale pink as she washed the blood off her legs. She had to dab them with a washcloth until she could bandage them again.

Her phone rang. She threw her clothes on and grabbed the phone off the dresser where she had not removed it from the armband from her run. A fight with the armband ensued to free her phone so she could answer it before they hung up.

"Hello."

Twenty-One

"HOW WAS YOUR RUN?" It was a male's voice she could only guess to be Tucker's, with how he sounded like a snake hissing into the phone.

Kassidy hung up. With a quick twist of her wrist, she threw her hair up into messy wet bun piled on top of her head. Maybe Detective Riggs could figure out how to keep Tucker from calling her. Disappointment clouded her face as she opened the back door: he was already gone. She called for the officer.

The officer moved up to the steps, where she informed him about the phone call. He keyed up his mic and let Detective Riggs know. She thanked him and spun on her heel to go back into her house.

"Ma'am, are you okay?" The officer gawked at her legs she hadn't finished bandaging. Fresh blood made a path down her legs from several of the punctures.

"Oh yeah, I'm going to re-bandage them now. Thanks." Embarrassed she closed the door behind her.

She grinned. Since he saw her out running, she knew he wasn't in her house. Band-Aids covered her legs in every which direction since she didn't have gauze and tape. She chuckled when she looked down at her legs. With a mop, bucket and cleaning supplies in hand, she felt her house was dirty with Tucker having been in who knew how many rooms. Maybe she could clean him out of her house and stop feeling violated by his presence in her home.

A couple of hours later, she had cleaned behind and under everything she wanted to and had worked up a sweat. This time after she showered, she grabbed her sweats and settled in to read the book she had started a couple of weeks ago but had never had the chance to finish. Although, first things first: she hadn't eaten yet so she thought about what she wanted for lunch.

As she sat down in the front room to eat, a shadow passed by her front door. She jumped and stifled a scream with her hand over her mouth. The uniform reminded her an officer was outside. The officer waved politely at her and stood back at his post. Nothing in his posture told her she had anything to worry about.

She felt guilty for taking so much of their time and stood back up to offer them lunch when another patrol car pulled up. That officer dropped off lunch for them.

She sat back down and ate in silence. Her stomach no longer growled so she picked up her book to read, only to realize she was tired. Maybe a quick twenty to thirty-minute nap would help. Kassidy curled up on her couch, as her eyes drooped, her breathing slowed. She slipped into unconsciousness.

With a quick look at the clock, she was shocked to see she had slept for almost two hours. Apparently, her lack of sleep was finally catching up to her. She went into a full body stretch and held it as long as she could. With the release of the stretch, her muscles returned to their normal buoyancy while she lay there for a whole minute and didn't move. Dishes clinked as she piled them on top of one another to carry them to the kitchen.

Maybe she would run down to the rental store and watch one of the newer movies that came out. With her purse slung over her shoulder and keys in her hand, she started out of the back door.

"I'm running a quick errand I'll be right back," Kassidy told the officer at the back of the house.

Once in the store, Kassidy headed straight to the new releases. She wasn't sure what movies from theaters were available to rent. The store had a musty smell she hadn't noticed before as she walked around and studied the covers. Interesting covers earned a read of the back cover. If both of those merited the desire to watch it, she then selected the movie to rent for the night.

With movies in hand, she was excited to see if the movies were as good as their jackets promised. Happily, she climbed the steps to the back deck and let herself in her house. She laid out a steak for dinner and thought about what to have with it. Her favorite marinade splashed around the steak in the glass dish as the different colors of the ingredients swirled together.

Movement out of the corner of her eye at the front door caught her attention as she put the disc in the Blu-ray player. This time she didn't jump since she remembered there was an officer out front also.

She enjoyed her evening of movies and steak, and several hours later, she headed to bed in hopeful anticipation of another night of uninterrupted sleep. She found she could barely keep her eyes from drooping, even after the nap she had taken that afternoon.

Twenty-Two

KASSIDY WOKE UP FEELING refreshed. She smiled to herself. She finally felt like her life was back to normal. With a quick glance around, nothing seemed out of place or missing. It had been several months but things appeared to be back to normal. The officers were no longer stationed outside her house. Tucker Miles still ranked number one on New Kingdom's most wanted but hadn't been seen anywhere in town.

It was thought that he had left when he realized he couldn't get to Kassidy anymore. Everyone had breathed a sigh of relief. Especially her! It was nice to be back in her room and not have the sense of foreboding like someone was watching her. Dark corners were no longer ominous warnings of his presence.

After she changed into her running gear, she sent her text to Sawyer to let him know her route. Since they were ready to move the case to the cold case file, he had asked if she would call him Sawyer. She liked that. Today would be the last day she sent a text of which route she would run. They had a felony warrant out for Tucker and she knew it was just a matter of time until another police department picked him up on it.

Officers checked on Tucker's house frequently, but with the dust that accumulated inside, they knew he hadn't been back there either.

A smile crept across her face as she saw Sawyer's reply to stay safe and that he would check in later. She took off at a good pace. No scary shadows skulked around corners.

About a mile into her run she slowed down as the hairs on the back of her neck stood up and bristled. She knew peering eyes watched her.

She did a 360-degree turn and looked every which direction but saw nothing. Now at a slower pace, she yanked her earbuds from her ears. She stopped mid-stride as she thought she heard footsteps. Maybe it hadn't been a good idea to come on the route she had this morning. It was a little way out of town and hardly any houses were out where she was. She spun as she heard footsteps. Frozen with fear, her pulse roared in her ears.

Her phone vibrated in her armband. A struggle ensued as she tried to remove her phone from her armband as her hands began to sweat and shake. A text from Sawyer asked her what was wrong.

She sent a text back telling him she had a weird feeling someone followed her.

He replied to get back home he would meet her there.

Before she could even register that she heard footsteps again, her scream was muffled as Tucker shoved something in her mouth. Her phone fell out of her hands as she grasped frantically for it but only came up with air. The screen shattered as it struck the ground.

She tried to hit and scratch him, but something was wrong. There was a bitter taste on whatever he had shoved in her mouth and her vision blurred as he placed duct tape over her mouth to keep whatever it was, in.

She fought to remove the duct tape, but he was stronger than she was. Now he had her hands behind her back as her vision faded. Fear gripped her chest and she wasn't sure Sawyer would get to her in time. But at least he would have a chance to find her since Tucker had left her fitness tracker on.

As the last of the light disappeared from her eyes, she tried to breathe through her nose but the darkness engulfed her. His strong arms were like a vice around her limp lifeless body as he picked her up to carry her away from her home. Her thoughts were of her friends who would never stop until Tucker was brought to justice.

Twenty-Three

SHE AWOKE WITH A START. Tucker still carried her. How long had she been out? Where had he taken her? How close was Sawyer to catching up to them? Tucker abruptly stopped and flipped her off his shoulder. Her head lolled to one side, so he held her up.

"Keep walking." It was back and meaner than ever.

It yanked her all over the place which caused her to stumble as she tried to keep up with how fast it wanted her to walk. Her shins hit a board and she winced but stopped herself from crying out. She didn't want to give it the satisfaction of hurting her. She looked up and gasped as her eyes focused, at least as much of a gasp that the duct tape allowed.

Four crudely made steps led up to a pole in the middle of a tiny platform. It spun her around and yanked off the duct tape. She cried out as a layer of her skin peeled off with the tape.

It had a satisfied look in its eyes as it grabbed the rope and pushed her back to the pole. The rope reeked of gasoline and her eyes grew wide. It was going to burn her alive. She closed her eyes. "My God is stronger than yours."

The sharp searing pain that started at her shoulder made her scream. With a snap of her head to the left, she saw what caused the pain. A look of pure horror spread across her face. It still had the same knife it had in the church. With that knife, it cut her arm from the shoulder down to her elbow.

An evil cackle erupted from Tucker's twisted mouth. It moved so Tucker's nose was almost touching hers. "Keep saying it and let me know how it works out for you. Because every time you say it, you will get more of that!"

Tuckers eyes were almost completely black and there was nothing but pure evil in them. She cried out as it bound her hands behind her back around the wooden post. She could feel blood pouring from her arm. Her lips moved as she silently prayed that if it was her time to be with her Heavenly Father, she would bleed-out before he set her on fire.

"Let's see if your God can get you out of this Kassidy." It sneered at her as it walked back around to face her. Tucker was not in control and she wondered if he even existed anymore.

It piled logs against the small platform, which was like the platforms they used to use during the witch trials when women were burned alive.

"My God is stronger than yours." She stated matter-of-factly. She didn't care what it had said earlier. It made her feel better to say it and she could feel God's love every time she did. If It burned her alive, she would make sure that statement was the last it would ever hear from her.

"No, He isn't," it sing-songed as it moved onto twigs and newspaper. It wadded up the newspaper and shoved it into every opening it could find between the larger logs.

"In Jesus' name, I bind you and demand you drop it!" She glared at it.

The bundle of twigs hit the ground and scattered. Its scream pierced the air as it picked them up one at a time.

"I told you my God is stronger than yours." Kassidy smiled and gazed toward Heaven.

"I dropped them; no one magically made me drop them. Shut up!" It collected the dropped twigs and walked back to the mountain of wood.

"In Christ Jesus' name, I command you to stop." She'd never sounded so calm. She knew the power in the name of Jesus, and if she wasn't mistaken the look on its face told her it did too.

It stopped mid-stride and seemed to struggle. Its face was a mixture of confusion and anger as it tried to figure out why it couldn't take another step forward. "Aaagghhhh!"

Kassidy saw lights in the distance. She knew one of those sets of lights would be Sawyer. The app he had her link her fitness band to on his tablet, apparently worked, because he was on his way to rescue her again. This demon wouldn't be happy to see him. She had to keep it busy until they could get to her; hopefully, before it lit the match.

To keep the attention on her so the demon that possessed Tucker didn't turn around and see the lights and speed up its timetable of burning her at the stake, she smiled down at it. "So, who magically made you stop this time?"

"Shut up!" Spit flew from its foaming mouth.

"My God is stronger than yours. He always has been, and He always will be. You know this, and your god knows this. There will come a time when every knee will bow, and every tongue will confess that my God is Lord."

The blackness in Tucker's eyes showed pure hatred when he looked at her. Fear no longer gripped her chest. She stared right back at Tucker. It struggled to take a step toward her. It failed.

But she knew she was running out of time. Light-headed from the blood loss, the world started to sway.

The lights grew brighter. Was that the roar of the police engines, gunned beyond their suggested limit that she heard?

It tilted its head to the side then snarled at her with such anger that it distorted Tucker's human face out of form. It spun around, enraged when it saw the police cars approach at breakneck speed. It spun back to her and threw the twigs haphazardly toward the pile of wood stacked around her. It sprinted out of the clearing and disappeared into the cornstalks as the first police car turned in from the road. A huge dust cloud kicked up as the police car's tires skidded, bringing it to a sudden stop. Sawyer was the first one out of the car. Huffman followed closely behind as he bolted out from the driver's seat.

"HE RAN TOWARDS THE south, right through the corn," Kassidy yelled, with as much energy as she could in spite of the blood loss.

Sawyer scrambled up past the wood and grabbed his knife. He cut the ropes that had cut into Kassidy's wrist and helped her down from what the demon had hoped to be her death-altar.

Huffman had left his vehicle behind for Sawyer and had taken other officers with him to search for Tucker. Kassidy had an eerie feeling he watched her as Sawyer pulled out a first aid kit to apply bandages to try and stop the bleeding. With her arm wrapped tightly, he cleaned her wrists from where the rope had cut the skin. The wrists weren't too bad with just minor abrasions. They would heal soon enough. The arm was another story. She would have a bad scar from the thick knife.

Someone stepped on a branch to the east and the snap cut through the quiet air. Sawyer pulled his gun so fast, Kassidy almost missed it and had it pointed in the direction of the noise. There were a couple more snaps before an officer broke through the rows of corn back to Sawyer and Kassidy's location.

"Anything?" Sawyer was tired of Tucker's game. He vowed this would be the last time that man would get hold of Kassidy if he had anything to do about it.

"Nothing. Sorry, sir. We saw tire marks; probably had a car waitin' just out of sight." The officer couldn't look Sawyer in the face as if he had let him down.

"Okay, I'll take her to the hospital. Grab another officer and immediately head over to her house and clear it to make sure he didn't get back into the attic." Sawyer nodded at Kassidy and opened the passenger door where she slid into the seat. Sawyer tossed the key to Kassidy's house to one of the officers who expertly caught it.

"Buckle up," Sawyer stated as he climbed into the driver's seat. The officer yelled for another officer who jumped into their police car and sped off toward her house.

The roar of the engine filled the car until it was drowned out by the sirens as Sawyer pushed the car well past the speed limit. "How's the arm?"

"To be honest, it's killing me. Sorry, no pun intended." Kassidy worried about how dirty the blade might have been. "How did you know something was wrong?"

"You slowed down and stopped. You've never once done that over the last couple of months we've tracked your runs."

"Nice to know you're so observant," Kassidy mumbled. She wanted to close her eyes. Warm blood seeped into the bandages.

"Oh, by the way, I have your phone. The only thing broken is the screen, so that's a good thing." Sawyer held up the phone from the driver's seat as they pulled into the hospital parking lot.

He practically hurdled the car to get to the passenger door for Kassidy. Henry stared at her as he pushed the stretcher from the back of his ambulance out of the hospital. Kassidy cringed as his eyes immediately went to her quickly bandaged arm through which the blood soaked.

"What happened now?" Henry scowled at Sawyer.

Twenty-Four

"IT WASN'T HIS FAULT," Kassidy stated, then walked into the hospital. Her arm hurt worse than she wanted to admit.

"Well then, whose fault is it?" Henry followed her.

"It's the demon who possessed Tucker," Kassidy said over her shoulder as she strolled up to the nurses' station.

"Kass, how bad's the arm?" Henry gingerly touched her on her non-injured shoulder.

"It hurts, worse than the nails."

Kassidy saw Henry flash a look at Sawyer.

"Hey, I got there as soon as I figured out something was wrong," Sawyer tried to explain.

"So, you knew something was wrong?" Henry raised an eyebrow at him.

"He can track my fitness tracker, so every time I run, he can watch where I am and know if something is wrong. Then he can find me by the GPS in my tracker." Kassidy sat down in a chair to fill out her paperwork. She thanked God it was her left arm he had cut instead of her right.

"So, he cut just your arm?"

"Are you going to tell him, or am I?" Sawyer asked.

"Yeah go ahead. I want to finish this form so I can get looked at and then get out of here."

Kassidy bent down over the clipboard and scribbled out the forms, while the nurse went to find a doctor.

"He tied her to a platform, to burn her alive," Sawyer said matter-of-factly.

"He what?" Henry snapped his head toward Kassidy.

"Shh, we're in a hospital." Kassidy didn't look up as she scrawled her signature on the form. She hurt too much to care about her penmanship.

She crossed over to the nurses' station just as a doctor walked out and asked for his next patient. The nurse took the clipboard from Kassidy then handed it directly to the doctor. The doctor turned to look at Kassidy with a smile.

"Hello doctor, how have you been?" Kassidy couldn't help but smile back; then grimaced.

"Well, let's go look at what we're dealing with this time." He walked to a curtain and held the corner back as she walked into an ER exam room. The corner of the curtain fell back into place, leaving Henry and Sawyer alone.

"Okay, let me get this bandage off." The doctor gently unwrapped her arm to remove the blood-soaked bandages. "Well, this doesn't look pretty. It doesn't look like they cut anything vital since several parts have started to clot."

"So, stitches or no stitches?" Kassidy already knew the answer but didn't want to stay for who knew how many stitches it might take to go from her shoulder to her elbow. She knew this wasn't going to be fixed with a box of band-aids.

"Do you want a plastic surgeon to stitch you up? I would suggest it with it being this bad of a cut." The doctor studied the wound then grabbed a syringe and injected her with a numbing agent. She turned her head. She didn't want to watch and felt dizzy as he irrigated the wound.

"How long to get him here?" she asked.

"Already have one upstairs. She finished up on a crash where a kid wasn't wearing a seatbelt and split his head open when he hit the windshield."

"No offense, but if she's already here, I'd love for her to stitch my arm," Kassidy smiled.

"Sure thing. Let me see if she's still down here." The doctor left the exam room, only to return a couple of minutes later with a female doctor in tow.

"Hello, I hear you need a few stitches." The female doctor came over and failed to hide her shock when she saw how ugly the cut was. "I'm sorry; we'll need to clean this out in surgery."

"Are you sure that's necessary?" Kassidy's head swam.

"Whoa, lay back." The doctors guided her back onto the bed. Then the first doctor stepped out from behind the curtain and asked the nurse to have an orderly get a gurney to take Miss Parker to O.R. 3.

"Doc, what's going on?" Fear crept across Sawyer's face.

Kassidy saw his expression from her bed.

"The cut's deep enough we don't know what kind of damage was done. It will be more comfortable for Miss Parker if we clean it out in a surgery room. We may also need to stitch inside the cut, Detective. This will take a while so we'll need to put her under to look at her muscles on that side of the arm. There may be internal damage that will need to be repaired in surgery. Nurse, please bring the paperwork she'll have to sign for surgery release." With that, the doctor disappeared back behind the curtain.

The nurse ambled over to the curtain with the forms for Kassidy to sign. Kassidy looked up at the doctors. She didn't want to be put under.

"We want to look around in there and see the damage to the muscles. Then we can decide from there how to repair it. It'll be a lot more comfortable for you if we do it while you're sedated. I don't think you want to be awake for what we have to do."

"Okay." Kassidy resigned herself to the fact she needed to go to surgery. She didn't want to take the chance she could lose some function in her arm. Nausea overwhelmed her at the thought of even glancing at her arm.

The nurse came back in and started an IV as an orderly rolled a gurney into her ER room. They helped her out of her clothes and into a hospital gown and placed her clothes in a bag. High-pitched squeaking came from the wheels as they pushed her out from behind the curtain.

Kassidy saw the concern on Sawyer's face as she was wheeled out of sight.

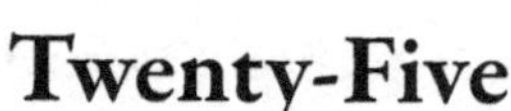

Twenty-Five

AN AGONIZING HOUR LATER, the doctor came into the O.R. waiting room to talk to Sawyer, who hadn't left after he was shown where he could wait for Kassidy.

"She's fine. By some miracle, the knife he used on her missed the muscles and did minimal damage inside. There should have been serious damage. It was a simple irrigate and suture procedure. You can take her home as soon as she wakes up a little more. She's still groggy. We'll also have prescriptions for pain and antibiotics already filled by the pharmacy here in the hospital."

The doctor shook Sawyer's outstretched hand.

"Detective, she's a strong young lady, but this better end." The doctor turned on his heels and left. Sawyer felt as if this one was no one's fault but his own. He should have realized with Tucker's infatuation with her he wouldn't just leave town. He slunk to the vending machine and bought a granola bar and a bottle of water. A little while later, they wheeled Kassidy out and the nurse gave her two prescription bottles. One was a painkiller and the other antibiotics. The nurse explained how to clean her arm and when to come back to get the stitches removed. Kassidy handed back the painkillers and thanked her then looked to Sawyer, who spoke with another officer.

"Are you ready to go?" Sawyer took a couple of awkward steps toward her. Her skin had a sickly pallor to it. She looked as if she might break. It took his breath away to see her like that.

"Yes, get me out of here."

He pushed Kassidy to the elevators.

They rode down in silence. Sawyer finally spoke as they crossed over the exit to the hospital. "I have the officers back at your house. I hope you don't mind, but when we used your key to clear the house, we left officers there to keep it secure and make sure he didn't return."

Sawyer opened the passenger car door for Kassidy as she slid in carefully, trying not to bump her arm.

Sawyer got in behind the wheel then turned over the engine. "Are you okay?"

"Yes. Thank you, for coming to save me yet again. I'm sorry you have to keep coming to find me." Kassidy leaned her head against the cool glass of the passenger window as Sawyer drove her home.

"Hey, I won't stop until he's behind bars or worse. I hate to say this but with it escalating, we'll more than likely have to kill him. Especially if he's ready to kill you like he tried to today."

"Thank you though. I really appreciate it." Kassidy turned from the window; tears threatened to spill over her red swollen eyes.

Sawyer placed his hand gently on the hand of her injured arm. "You're welcome."

They felt an attraction and had talked about it before. She explained it was against her faith to date anyone who didn't believe the same she did. He said he understood, but he wasn't ready to take the leap to be where she was in her faith. Slowly he read the Bible she'd given him. They talked about the things he read, but it was so hard to accept when it said he was a sinner and no one gets to Heaven just by doing good things.

He liked the parts that talked about God's love and how forgiving He was with His people when He led them out of Egypt. How He always gave them so many chances to come back to Him. He could definitely get on board with a God who was that forgiving, yet He still gave them the free choice to make that decision themselves.

Kassidy closed her eyes, leaned her head back and whispered. "My God is stronger than his."

Sawyer glanced at her but said nothing. He was attracted to her for her strong belief in her God and how she never faltered from that conviction; someone who was that open yet didn't look down on others who didn't believe the same way. She really made him think maybe she was right. How she dealt with this ordeal she was going through with prayer and how she prayed for Tucker whom she said was possessed, shocked him. How could someone pray for someone who hurt them?

She explained that it's hard to be mad at someone you're praying for. It made little sense to him but she believed it. She said she worried for his soul since he was possessed. Sawyer had to admit he was starting to believe the possession part. Tucker's different eye colors and the changes in his voice —there was something to the changes in his demeanor; it was something Sawyer had never seen before.

His main concern was how far he would go to get Kassidy before they caught him. He seemed to be one step ahead of them. It didn't seem possible that someone could plan that far ahead. Maybe he was getting help from this demon. Wait, was he seriously considering this possession that Kassidy talked about? If he was, then he would have to consider what the Bible said was true. As she said, you either accept the entire Bible or you believe none of it. There's no belief of this part yet not the other. It's all the same book. That would be the same as the dictionary. You don't believe only some of the definitions and not others.

He pulled into her driveway as Kassidy lifted her head.

"Are you okay?" Sawyer studied her face. She hadn't said a word on the drive to her house.

"YEAH, JUST TIRED. THEY gave me something for pain when they stitched me up. I think that's what's making me so tired." Kassidy opened the car door and half smiled at the officer at the back of her house. She felt so bad that this was their detail yet again.

"Is there anything I can get you?" Sawyer gazed through his mirrored sunglasses at her.

"No thanks. I'm just going to lie down. Is there anything I can do for these men who are keeping my house secure? I feel horrible that this is what they do all day and night." Kassidy half turned back toward Sawyer.

"No, with this small of a town we have plenty of manning. They volunteer for this duty. They want to catch him, as much as you and I want him caught."

"They volunteer? But why? They don't know me."

"Some like the easy assignment and others can't stand what he's put you through. They take their jobs seriously, and their main concern isn't only you but all the citizens of New Kingdom."

"Well, let them all know, who have been out here, it means the world to me. Thank you so much." Kassidy trudged up the stairs to her house and let herself in the back door.

With her back pressed against the door, she realized this needed to end so she wouldn't feel so afraid in her own home. Her lips mouthed silent words in prayer for strength to get through it and that this demon was quickly stopped. She made her way to the living room, curled up on the couch, covered herself with her favorite throw then fell asleep.

Several hours later she woke. Her arm ached and had bled through a little on the bandages. In the kitchen, she picked up what she thought were the prescription pain pills the doctor had given her in the hospital then dropped it back onto the counter. She remembered the last time she took prescription pain meds how dizzy and groggy they had made her. She didn't want to deal with that again, so she grabbed generic pain relievers and downed four with a glass of water. She shuffled down the hall to the master bathroom. The bottom drawer was a stockpile of gauze and bandage rolls, which she helped herself to as she contemplated how to change her bandage.

She scrunched her nose at the grotesque wound when she took the old bandages off. She hoped she wouldn't scar too bad but the plastic surgeon who had been on duty had done a meticulous job and kept the stitches small and closely grouped together.

Her stomach growled, so she looked at the clock. She'd slept through lunch and it was now late enough to get an early dinner. She was hungry but wasn't sure what she wanted to eat.

On the way down the hallway, she heard her phone ring and jogged to the kitchen. In a scramble to get it out of her purse, she remembered it had a shattered screen. Celeste's name showed through the distorted shards of glass. With hesitation, she remembered last time she thought it was Celeste, and it was wasn't.

No, she shook her head, she wouldn't be afraid to answer her own phone. She could always hang up on Tucker if it was him.

"Hello." Kassidy was proud of her steady voice.

"Hey, what're you doing for dinner? Henry and I want to go to Sammy's." It was Celeste.

"Sammy's sounds great. I'm starved." Kassidy smiled.

"Great, we'll pick you up in twenty minutes."

Kassidy jogged down the hall to her bathroom. After she ran a brush through her hair, she brushed her teeth. With all the blood on her clothes, she realized, she'd have to change. Celeste would panic if she saw her like this.

Icy cold water filled the sink as she placed her blood-soaked shirt in the cold water to soak while she went out to dinner. After a quick five-minute shower, she realized how hard it was to not get a bandage wet in the shower. She threw on clothes as her doorbell rang.

Twenty-Six

A SMILING CELESTE, who gawked at her through the glass in the back door, made Kassidy laugh as she finished putting on the plaid shirt she had grabbed from her closet. She grabbed her ID, some cash and keys. After a quick hug with Celeste, she saw that Henry was in the driver's seat of the car.

"I'm starved. Let's go." A quick jiggle of the door handle told Kassidy her house was secure. Celeste skipped down the stairs as Kassidy trailed her.

"Yeah, Henry didn't get to eat lunch today from working a crash. You know how fun he is when he doesn't get to eat," Celeste laughed as she opened the passenger door.

Kassidy simultaneously opened the back door and they both slid into the car in perfect harmony.

"Oh yeah, that's scary."

"What's scary?" Henry glanced between the two girls.

"Oh, nothing." Both girls roared with laughter.

"Yeah, if you say so. I don't trust it when you both answer at the same time and then laugh."

Henry put the car in reverse, threw his arm over the back of the passenger seat, and then watched out the back window as he backed out of the driveway. He steered the car toward their favorite restaurant.

"You know us too well. So, Henry said you had another incident today?" Celeste didn't turn around.

"Yes, but I'm okay. Sawyer, I mean Detective Riggs, got there before it could do anything."

Kassidy watched the scenery pass.

"Sawyer?" Celeste turned around with raised eyebrows and smiled.

"Stop it. You know we've been talking. I really think I'm making headway with him about God. I'm hopeful about his acceptance that what the Bible says is true."

Kassidy knew it was better not to hide anything from her friends; they'd known each other too long to keep secrets.

"Wow, really, that's great. Is he going to come to church on Sundays?" Celeste faced forward again.

"I don't think he's ready for that yet. He did seem to be open about several things in the Bible I've had him read though."

"Well, I think you guys would be great together. You would make an adorable couple."

"And you two know what the Bible says about unequally yoked." Kassidy peered at the back of her friend's head as if to bore a hole in it.

"Oh Hun, I know. I'm just saying if it looks promising, Henry and I couldn't be happier. When we came to this quaint little town after you told us how great it was, I hoped it was because of a guy you'd met. So now years later, knowing you may have met a great guy, it makes me happy." She smiled back at Kassidy.

"I appreciate that. Let's not get me married just yet though. We haven't even gone out on a date. And we won't until they catch Tucker."

"Okay. Speaking of, are you not going to tell me how he wanted to burn you alive today?" Celeste had turned back around and was fumbling with the zipper on her purse.

"Detective Riggs got there in time and I'm okay. Everyone thought he'd left, but now we know he doesn't scare off that easy. He's stepped up the house watch, and I won't go anywhere without someone with me." Her voice shook as tears threatened to fall.

"Well good. Is there anything we can do to help? I hate that you're staying in that house by yourself. I know, I know, you don't want to give him the power that he's scared you out of your home."

"Yeah, you can help me get a treadmill and put it together since they weigh more than I do." Kassidy changed the subject and hoped that would be the end for tonight.

"Oh, gee manual labor. I see how you treat your best friends." Celeste nudged Henry who had kept quiet so far.

"I'm game. We'll have to do it when I have my truck though." Henry pulled into Sammy's and they all shuffled out of the car.

With the subject changed they went in to have a nice quiet dinner.

The conversation was light and upbeat. They joked about childhood stories. Kassidy loved to spend time with her friends. She was glad they'd moved to New Kingdom after she told them about the town and the great church she'd found.

Kassidy picked up the tab and paid for all their meals. "Do you mind if we get the treadmill today?"

"Sure, I have no plans and Henry's off for forty-eight hours. We need to pick up the truck though." Celeste studied Kassidy, then leaned toward her, but didn't say anything about her pale color.

"My arm hurts. Do you mind if we stop by a drugstore to pick up aspirin or something?"

"Why didn't you say something? I have some." Celeste's hands disappeared as she dug around in the over-sized purse that usually contained everything except a kitchen sink. After a moment, she produced a bottle of Tylenol.

"Thanks." Kassidy downed two pills dry then handed the bottle back.

"Okay, let's grab the truck." Henry slid behind the wheel.

They rode in silence to get the truck since they were full from dinner. Once they all transferred over to the truck, they discussed where the best place to pick up a treadmill would be. All agreed on the local department store. It was harder than she thought it would be to decide on a treadmill. In the end, she settled for the weekly sale deal which also had the most options.

A store employee helped Henry load it into the back of the truck while the girls supervised. Kassidy held her arm protectively close to her body. Small beads of sweat collected on her forehead as they drove back to her house.

Surprised to see Sawyer in the driveway with the officer posted to watch the back door, her heart dropped. What had happened now? She opened the door to drop down out of the truck then made a beeline for Sawyer.

"Is there something going on?" Kassidy was joined by Celeste and Henry.

"No, I was just checking in. Sorry, didn't mean to make you think something had happened."

"Good, perfect timing. We need to implore you for help," Henry smirked at Kassidy.

"Oh no, it's okay we can get it." She couldn't believe Henry would ask Sawyer to help carry in the treadmill.

"Sure, what's going on?" Sawyer raised an eyebrow as a grin played at the corners of his mouth.

"Well, Kass bought a treadmill and I don't want her to help carry it in and pull her stitches."

Henry walked back to the truck then lowered the heavy tailgate before he hopped into the bed of the truck to release the straps.

"I absolutely agree. I was going to suggest a treadmill if you wanted to keep running. It'll keep you safe and off the road while Tucker's out there lurking around." Sawyer joined Henry at the bed of the truck.

"Come on; let's get the door for them. Oh hey, where are we putting it anyway?" Celeste hooked her arm through Kassidy's good arm.

"I was going to put it in the basement family room so it's out of the way." Kassidy cringed. Was it asking too much for the guys to carry it not only into her house but also down a flight of stairs into the basement?

"Officer, help us for a minute." Sawyer didn't ask but suggested they would need help.

The officer smiled and scrambled to the back of the truck. "Sure."

Celeste held the back door open as Kassidy turned on lights in the hallway then opened the basement door. She hurried down the stairs to turn on the lights and make sure they had a clear path. Before she crested the top of the basement stairs, the guys came up the back stairs. Kassidy stepped to the side as Henry guided them toward the stairs to the basement and they carried the treadmill down with ease. Muscles strained under their shirts and pushed the fabric to its limits. Kassidy's jaw dropped at Sawyers well-defined arms. Celeste nudged Kassidy after she closed the back door and laughed.

"Stop it." Heat flushed Kassidy's face and neck.

"Not bad, Kass." Celeste continued down the basement stairs followed by a still blushing Kassidy.

"Over behind the table if you could." Kassidy directed them where it would be the most out of the way yet easily accessible.

"Look good?" Henry asked as they set the box down next to where she wanted the treadmill.

"Perfect—then I won't have to move it much when I put it together." Kassidy couldn't even think about that tonight.

"Oh, put it together?! Not on your life with your arm the way it is." Sawyer glowered.

"I'll be at my post," the officer smirked as he quickly excused himself. He took the stairs two at a time, taking him far away from the possible argument that was about to ensue.

"No, Detective Riggs, you've done more than enough to help. I'm very handy with tools and can put this together myself." Kassidy opened a closet door, then pulled out a good-sized toolbox and gestured to it.

"Nope, you heard the Detective. You don't get to put this together. Hun, grab me some water if you would please." Henry flashed a smile at his wife.

"Sure. Detective?"

"That would be great." Sawyer unclipped his holster and badge. He set them on the top of a bookshelf close to the treadmill and rolled up his sleeves.

"Detective, we can get this." Sweat ran down Kassidy's temple as she unconsciously swiped at it.

"Hey, are you okay? You look flushed." Sawyer took a step toward her. His iron grip gingerly took the toolbox from her.

"Yes, I'm fine. It's just a little warm."

Kassidy turned and closed the closet door. Dizzy as she turned back around, she stumbled a couple of steps in an attempt to stay upright. Sawyer and Henry rushed to her and helped her sit in a chair. Henry immediately took her pulse, the ever-ready paramedic. She couldn't understand why she was so hot.

"What happened?" Celeste stopped at the bottom of the stairs with two glasses of water.

"I don't feel good. Maybe I'll lie down for a couple minutes then come back and help you guys."

"Kass, you're running a fever. Did you take the antibiotics they would have given you at the hospital?" Henry removed his hand from her forehead.

"I think all they gave me were pain pills and I haven't taken any of them."

"You said no to pain pills, so they only gave you antibiotics. Didn't you see that on the label?" Sawyer placed his hand on her wounded arm on the side of the chair where he stood. His cool hand felt good on her feverish skin. Infection had set in.

"I'll get them. Where are they, Kass?" Water sloshed out of the glasses as Celeste set them on the coffee table then started up the stairs.

"They're on the kitchen counter by the bread box. I didn't read the label." Kassidy whispered the last.

Celeste came down the steps before Kassidy had even blinked. "Oh, I forgot the water."

"Here." Ice clinked against the side of the glass as Sawyer grabbed it from the table then handed it to Kassidy. Henry perused the label on the bottle then gave one pill to Kassidy.

"Thanks." Kassidy vaguely remembered handing a bottle back to the nurse but didn't recall the conversation they'd had about it.

"Now go lie down; we'll take care of this." Concern etched Sawyer's face. He stared at her as she walked upstairs.

Celeste held on to Kassidy's right side to make sure she was stable enough to walk up the stairs. Kassidy could hear one of the two guys open the toolbox and another cut open the corrugated cardboard box that encased the treadmill.

"Seriously Kass, how did you make that mistake? You never do things like that." Celeste guided her to the couch in the living room then grabbed a blanket.

"I don't know. I can't believe I was that dumb." Kassidy lay back to close her eyes just for a moment and was asleep before Celeste walked back to the basement stairs.

"HENRY, SHE DOESN'T look good. Do you think she has an infection?" Celeste asked from the bottom of the basement stairs.

"More than likely. We can always take her back to the hospital and get a booster shot of antibiotics but I'm not sure she'll go for that." Henry had the box open for the treadmill.

"Yeah, she won't. She hates hospitals," Sawyer muttered matter-of-factly.

"We'll keep an eye on her for the next few hours and see if anything changes. If not then we'll take her back to the hospital. She can't fight all three of us on that." Henry winked at Sawyer.

Celeste grabbed the set of instructions and set out all the nuts and bolts that were packaged with the treadmill. She gave directions on how to assemble the treadmill. They worked well together, figured out the confusing parts of the instructions and had the treadmill together in no time. Sawyer put the tools away; then he and Henry moved the treadmill to where Kassidy had first instructed she wanted it.

Sawyer clipped his badge and holster back onto his belt. He had barely worked up a sweat by the time they all headed upstairs to check on Kassidy who was still asleep on the couch. Henry checked her pulse and made sure her breathing was okay.

"I don't want to wake her or leave her alone. Do you mind if I stay here with her tonight, babe?" Celeste couldn't take her eyes off Kassidy.

"Sure, no problem. I'll pick you up tomorrow and bring breakfast." Henry kissed Celeste on the top of the head and walked through the kitchen to the back door.

Sawyer stood in the living room and watched Kassidy sleep. She looked so small and frail. He knew she wasn't like that normally and it scared him in a way he didn't like. He knew his feelings were growing toward Kassidy, but first and foremost he had a job to do.

"I'll stay." The words were out before he could stop himself.

"Are you sure?" Celeste cringed at what Kassidy would say when she woke up with him there instead of her or Henry.

"If something goes wrong, I can get her to the hospital faster than you could. I have a police car." He smirked at Celeste.

"Henry, wait up; we'll bring all of us breakfast in the morning." Celeste joined Henry at the back door. He raised his eyebrows at his wife.

"Detective Riggs will stay with her. We'll bring breakfast tomorrow—enough for all four of us." Celeste grabbed her husband's hand and squeezed.

Sawyer saw that they were just as concerned as he was.

"You know she'll kill us for leaving him with her instead of one of us," Henry whispered as they closed the back door. They waved to the officer as they jumped in their truck.

Sawyer stole to the back door then motioned the officer over. "Yes, sir?"

"I'll stay here for a bit. She may have an infection from the cut on her arm; she can't be alone. Can you run down to the store and grab me a salad?" Sawyer hated to ask, but he didn't want to leave Kassidy alone to run down to the store himself.

"Yes, sir. Did you want me to have someone relieve me?"

"No, I'll stay at the back door until you get back." Sawyer took out some cash and told the officer what he wanted.

The officer was gone only a few minutes. When he pulled back into the driveway, Sawyer met him at the bottom of the steps. "Thanks."

"Is she going to be okay?" The officers who worked her detail wanted Tucker so bad, they could taste it.

"Should be but I'll let you know if we need to have her transported." Sawyer closed then locked the back door behind him. As quietly as possible, he snuck into the front room to eat while he kept an eye on Kassidy.

Kassidy's phone rang. Sawyer wasn't sure if he should answer it or let it go to voicemail. He didn't want it to wake her up. He picked it up and saw that it said, Celeste. He figured she wanted to know how Kassidy was doing.

"Hello?" Sawyer quietly answered.

"Hello?" Sawyer raised his voice.

"What are you doing answering her phone?" It was a male's voice.

"Who's this?" Sawyer knew it wasn't Henry.

"Wait! Are you in her house?" Anger seeped through the phone.

"Tucker?" Sawyer tensed as he stood, his hand instinctively dropped to his gun.

"You get away from my girl!" Tucker hissed.

"She isn't your girl, Tucker and she never will be. We'll catch you and you'll go to jail for a very long time." Sawyer turned a full circle then relaxed when nothing seemed to arouse his suspicions.

"Yes, she is! She'll be mine or she won't be anyone's! You may be her rescuer right now but I am who she was meant for. She'll never be yours!" Tucker slammed the phone down.

Sawyer glanced over at Kassidy who still slept and he promised himself he would get her through this. She would never know about this phone call and he would do everything physically possible to never let him hurt her again.

He studied Kassidy for a second when he realized he couldn't tell if she was breathing. He lunged to the edge of the couch and felt for a pulse as his heart raced. A sigh of relief escaped louder than he intended as he hung his head so that it almost rested on her shoulder. Her pulse was strong.

Kassidy's phone rang again. He snatched it off the table. It read Celeste on the caller ID.

"Hello?"

"Hey is she still asleep?" It was Celeste.

"Yes, her pulse is strong, but she's so pale," Sawyer told Kassidy's best friend.

"Well, we're getting ready to go to bed. Let us know if anything changes. We can be there in a couple of minutes."

"Okay, sounds good. Talk to you later."

The house grew darker as the sun set in the distance. He slipped his shoes off then settled back into the recliner. He watched Kassidy sleep until he could keep his eyes open no longer and he slipped into a restless sleep.

Sawyer sat straight up at the edge of the chair and waited for his eyes to adjust to the darkness. A glance at the couch told him Kassidy wasn't there. As he stood, the blanket that had covered him fell to the ground. The coolness of the house made him shiver.

He tried to fit the pieces together when he realized she must have covered him when she woke up. Unable to see his watch, he tried to figure out what time it was. As he tiptoed down the hall toward her room, he ran his hand down the wall to tell him where the hall ended and her doorway started. When she didn't answer his knock, he tried the doorknob and was relieved when he found it unlocked.

He wanted to check on her but didn't want to scare her or wake her up. In a timid whisper, he said her name. She didn't stir. A check of her pulse and he found it steady and strong. With a sigh of relief, he closed her door then blindly walked back to the living room, hands out in front of him. Settled into the recliner he closed his eyes again but he couldn't fall back to sleep.

Twenty-Seven

AROUND FOUR THIRTY Kassidy wandered down the hall and smiled sheepishly at Sawyer who stood up from the recliner.

"Are you feeling better?" Sawyer asked.

"Yes. Thanks for staying—you didn't need to. I would've been okay." Kassidy walked into the kitchen and filled her tea kettle.

"You still look pale though."

"Do I?" Kassidy touched her face with her hand as if feeling her face would tell her if she was pale or not.

"Sorry to say, yes."

"I'm sorry I fell asleep. I can't believe I slept that long." Kassidy opened her prescription for antibiotics and took another dose with milk. "Did you want something to eat?"

"Henry said something about bringing breakfast over this morning when they come over. I have to go home; then go into the department to look into a few things. I need to see if any new developments came in overnight." Sawyer stepped toward the back door. He half turned to her but then left without another word.

Kassidy made tea and went back down the hall to her bathroom to jump in the shower in an attempt to make herself appear less pale. She felt better and hoped that meant the antibiotics were working. With a look in the mirror, she sighed. The mirror didn't lie: she looked like death warmed over. No matter what, nothing would help the pale skin and the dark under the eyes go away.

Remembering her treadmill, she decided to see how it looked. She felt bad that the guys had done all the work, and she hadn't even been conscious of it. The treadmill looked huge in the basement. She didn't remember it looking this big on the floor in the department store.

As she stood on it, she wasn't sure she would like using this instead of running outside. She wanted to keep running and knew she wouldn't be able to with Tucker still out there stalking her. Stalking her! That thought made her shudder as if the temperature had dropped twenty degrees. The treadmill could wait until tomorrow. She would give herself another day to rest and hopefully be back to almost one hundred percent by then.

The doorbell rang as she climbed the last stair. It shocked her that they were up this early. They usually weren't up before seven am. She unlocked the door and was greeted by the delicious aroma of bacon, biscuits, eggs and hash browns.

"Gee, what did you bring? Your whole kitchen?"

"I think we did." Henry pulled food out of several bags.

"You don't look so good. How are you feeling?" Celeste grabbed Kassidy by both shoulders and looked her square in the eye. She was gentle with the injured shoulder.

"Actually, I feel a lot better. I just don't look any better." Kassidy gave her a quick hug then grabbed plates out of the cabinet along with glasses. Celeste had already grabbed silverware before Kassidy could suggest it.

"Did you take more this morning?" Henry frowned.

"Yes sir, I did. I don't have to take more until this afternoon." Kassidy's scowl caused Henry to smile.

"Where's Detective Riggs?" Celeste looked around questioningly.

"He had to get to work. He left a little while ago." Kassidy wouldn't meet their eyes. Instead, she dug through the food to see what they had brought. Everything smelled so good and she was starved.

"So, he stayed the night?" Celeste asked innocently.

"Yes, he was asleep in the recliner when I woke up around three. I went to bed and slept until four thirty. Couldn't go back to sleep so figured I'd slept enough. He then left after I woke up and said something about things he had to work on and follow-ups to complete."

"Well, he'd better be following up on how to catch Tucker and put him in jail. I'm not sure you can take much more of this, to be honest." Celeste had nothing but love in her eyes.

Kassidy loved Celeste and Henry more than anything. They were her family whether they were related by blood or not. "Let's eat. I'm famished."

"Deal." Henry grabbed his plate and let Kassidy and Celeste fix their breakfast first then followed them into the dining room to sit down at the table Kassidy hardly ever used.

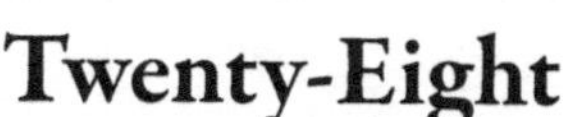

Twenty-Eight

THEY ATE IN SILENCE and then, after they cleared the table from their delicious breakfast, they migrated to the living room to discuss what they would do for the day. Henry had to work the next day so they wouldn't make plans that ran too late since he had to work at six in the morning.

"Hey, there's something we'd like to talk about." Celeste reached for Henry's hand.

"Sure, what's going on?" Kassidy could see how in love they still were after all their years together.

"Well, we wanted you to be the first to know, we're gonna have a baby." Celeste beamed.

"What?" Kassidy almost yelled.

"You heard me. I'm not far along so we haven't told anyone, but I'm definitely pregnant. We couldn't be happier." Henry pecked Celeste's cheek.

"But the doctors said you couldn't have kids." Kassidy was shocked to say the least, but happier than she could express for her best friends.

Celeste burst out laughing. "Well, our God is stronger than theirs."

Kassidy and Celeste jumped up and hugged for what seemed like minutes. Then Kassidy gave Henry an enormous hug. They would make great parents. This little baby would have more love than it would know what to do with.

"I'm so happy for you guys. When are you due?" Kassidy had so many ideas already about a baby shower. There was so much love they would give the little person who grew inside her best friend.

"I'm only a few months along so I still have a long way to go. But we have never been happier." Celeste and Henry wrapped their arms around each other.

Kassidy's phone rang. They exchanged confused looks; she usually only got calls from one of them, since she had no family left.

She laughed and showed Celeste her phone. "Look you're calling me."

"Wait. What?" Celeste took Kassidy's phone and sure enough, it showed her name and phone number on the caller ID.

Kassidy took the phone back and slid her finger over the reject button.

"Wait, you know who it is, don't you?" Henry had that protective look he had around her lately ever since her first encounter with Tucker.

"It's him. He makes his calls look like they're coming from you." Kassidy set her phone down on the end table.

"Are you serious? How do you know when it's actually me calling?"

"I don't. I usually answer then hang up if it's him." Kassidy didn't like that he'd touched so much of the good in her life and made her afraid in her own home.

"Well then change my name in your contact list so you know it's me, until they catch him." Celeste smiled.

"Good idea. But what can I change it to?" Kassidy already knew she would put 'mommy2b' as the contact name. With a quick couple of taps on her phone, she changed it then showed Celeste and Henry the screen. Laughter echoed through the house.

"I say we get out of here for a little bit. Do you feel like visiting the local department store to see what they have in the baby section?" Celeste glowed and Kassidy didn't know why she hadn't seen it until now. Her friend was even more beautiful than usual.

"I think that's a great idea!" Kassidy grabbed her phone to throw it in her purse. She locked the back door while Celeste and Henry started down the stairs to their car.

They walked for the next two hours through the baby section and looked at everything the department had to offer. Henry even got into it. He had so many suggestions and ways he wanted to decorate the room. They had both discussed it and didn't want to know what they were having; they wanted it to be a surprise when the delivery came.

They agreed to drop Kassidy off first since she was tired and needed to take another dose of antibiotics. She told them a nap was also in order. Henry needed to do a couple of things around the house before his shift started the next day and Celeste wanted to think about what room they would make into the baby's room and how to arrange it.

Kassidy jumped out of the car at her house then let herself in through the back door. Celeste and Henry waved as they backed out of the driveway. Kassidy couldn't wipe the huge grin off her face; she couldn't have been happier for them. Her phone rang, and she pulled it out of her purse and cracked up at Celeste's new name. "Hey."

"Hey, wanted to see if we could get together tomorrow after church since Henry will be at work and we can talk baby stuff." Celeste laughed at something Henry said in the background.

"That would be great; sounds like a plan," Kassidy laughed.

Henry could be heard saying in the background that those two together all afternoon could only lead to trouble.

The next dose of antibiotics was on its way through her system. She walked down the hallway to her room and thought a nap sounded perfect. Her shoes were set by the side of the bed. She fell asleep in a matter of minutes with her covers tucked securely around her.

The doorbell woke her with a start. Sawyer stood at her back door and she felt suddenly self-conscious about how bad she would look since she had just woken up.

"What's wrong?" She ran her fingers through her hair trying to tame her locks.

"Have you seen the officer that was posted at your back door?" Sawyer's voice was strained. Kassidy had never heard him like that before.

"No, and now that you mention it, I don't think he was here when I got home after going out with Celeste and Henry."

"What time was that?" Sawyer had his mic keyed and asked for the officers that were already enroute to step it up.

"I'm not sure. It was before noon. What time is it now? I fell asleep when I got home."

"It's almost fourteen-thirty, sorry two-thirty." Sawyer keyed up his radio. "Yes. Get the officers out here now. Officer Rollins is missing. Last seen at least three hours ago." Sawyer scanned the area.

Kassidy worried Tucker was to blame. Could Tucker be that dumb to hurt an officer, or worse? The entire police department would be out for blood.

"Do you think Tucker...?" Kassidy's voice trailed off before she finished the sentence.

"I wouldn't put it past him. If he's hurt one of my guys, we'll scour the entire city until we find him. I hate to be blunt, but he may not be taken alive if certain officers get a hold of him first." Sawyer watched Kassidy's reaction.

"He didn't get in my house, did he?" Kassidy spun on her heels and put her back to Sawyer as she peered warily into her house.

With both hands on her shoulders, he steered her so she was behind him. "Stay here, I want to check first." Sawyer didn't wait for more officers but drew his gun.

"I'm not staying out here by myself. You're crazy if you think that." Kassidy glued herself to his side.

"You won't be alone. I'll have Officer Phelps at the front door stay with you." Sawyer was already halfway to the front door.

"How about he stays here and watches the front and back doors and I'll follow you." Kassidy innocently smiled up at Sawyer.

"Phelps, stay here and keep an eye on the front and back door while I clear the house." Sawyer started down the hallway, gun raised slightly.

Kassidy stayed several steps behind him. He cleared the rooms one by one. She stayed in the doorway of each room to keep an eye on him. She wasn't sure she could do much, but if something happened, she could yell for Phelps.

Now that the master bedroom was cleared he motioned her to the doorway that led to the bathroom until he could get into the attic. She pictured Tucker lurking up there. What if he was waiting for Sawyer and hurt him? Her hand went to her throat at the thought of Sawyer hurt. She'd gotten used to having him around.

Quietly, with the access panel open, he peeked into the attic. The farther he continued into the dark recesses of the attic, the faster her heart raced. Seconds ticked by as her clock in the bathroom alerted her with every jump of the second hand. A bright beam from Sawyer's flashlight flashed over the opening. His feet found the rungs of the ladder and he descended back into her world, safe and unharmed.

"Anything?" Kassidy reached out to touch his arm but pulled her hand back before he saw it.

"Nothing." He went back down the hall as the first set of officers arrived. The alley to her house looked like a police convention was about to begin, with cars parked every possible direction.

"Where do we start?" Huffman barked. She decided she never wanted to be on Huffman's bad side.

"Set a perimeter. County K-9 should be here in the next few minutes." Sawyer started toward Rollins' car that he had driven that day. The officers couldn't take their eyes off Sawyer as he popped the trunk and lifted the lid. Nothing.

Kassidy didn't want to know if he was in the trunk and was glad Tucker wasn't back in her house. She prayed that Rollins be found quickly and that he wasn't hurt or worse.

"Kassidy, stay in your house. Lock the door since we know he isn't inside and don't come out until I come back. I'll let you know what we've found. Officer Marks, you are now on the post at the back door. He doesn't get to her. Do you understand? I don't care what force you have to use but he does not get to her." Sawyer pointed at Kassidy.

Kassidy closed the door behind her, leaned her head against the door and whispered. "My God is stronger."

County's K-9 deputy pulled up on the street and let out probably one of the largest, fiercest dogs she'd ever seen. She hoped the dog was good enough to find Rollins fast. Dusk was in just a couple of hours, and she didn't want the sun to set before he was found.

She watched the county deputy tell the K-9 to track. The dog took off with a leap. Two officers paced with the K-9 but at a few strides behind him so they didn't interfere with the track. Past a grove of trees across the alley from her house, they disappeared through the brush. She knew the wooded area wasn't that large, but she didn't like the thought of the officers being in there with Tucker still on the loose, especially Sawyer. She snatched her phone off the counter and called Celeste. Once the officers were added to the prayer chain for a quick and safe return for everyone including Rollins, she breathed easier.

Time ticked by as she watched the clock on the stove. With every ten minutes, her heart sank as she paced back and forth the length of the kitchen island. Fierce barking in the distance broke the deadly silence as she jerked her head toward the woods. She prayed the K-9 had found Tucker. She strained to hear if anyone yelled from an attack from the dog. Nothing pierced the confines of her home. The sun sank lower in the sky to cast long deep shadows through the trees.

The cooler bounced up the steps from the garage as she yanked it into the kitchen. Ice thudded into the cooler and scattered every direction as Kassidy dumped the ice tray from the freezer into it. Bottles of water were placed in the cooler so they'd be ready for the officers when they got back. It was a warm day with the sun out.

Several agonizing minutes ticked by before she heard the wail of the sirens from an ambulance in the distance. "Father, please let everyone be okay." She cried in earnest.

Officer Marks knocked on the back door and startled her from her prayer. She took a swipe at her tears before she opened the back door.

"Yes."

"Detective Sawyer wanted me to let you know they found Rollins. He's injured but looks like he'll make it. The detective said it'll be a while before he can make it back to the house but he wanted you to know." The tensed muscles in Officer Marks' face relaxed and the creases in his forehead diminished as he told her.

"Thank you so much. I have water for everyone." Kassidy rolled the cooler out to Officer Marks so he could take it down to the driveway.

"Thank you, that's very nice. They'll really appreciate it." Officer Marks carried it down the steps then placed it in the driveway.

Kassidy locked the door then called Celeste to give her the update. She cried as she told her.

After she hung up, she looked outside to see the first officers come back drenched with sweat that darkened their uniforms. They gladly helped themselves to the water that was in the cooler. Each officer took a bottle and readily drank half of it before they brought it away from their mouths.

Huffman and the county K-9 were the last ones to arrive and the deputy opened a bottle and popped out a portable bowl for the dog to drink from. The dog lapped up the water greedily as saliva strung from his frothy mouth. The deputy emptied the rest of his bottle into the bowl for the dog to finish. He waved up to Kassidy to thank her. She raised her hand in answer and felt it just wasn't enough.

Huffman made his way to the back door. She had it open before he could knock.

"Riggs wanted me to let ya know a little more detail on what happened. Apparently, accordin' to Rollins, Tucker came by after you left with your friends. The officer saw him in the tree line and took off after him. He should've called for backup instead of leavin' his post. Tucker waited for him and knocked him out; dragged him a good distance before he stabbed him."

Kassidy's gasp caused Huffman to pause.

"Is he going to be okay?" A tear slid down Kassidy's cheek.

Huffman continued in a hushed, calm voice. "They think he'll be okay. He was awake and talkin' the whole time after we found him. He said he got a shot off and may have hit Tucker. We'll call the local hospitals an' see if he checked himself in. The K-9 tracked him to where we found tire tracks so he got into a car. Riggs said you're not to leave your house tonight and to make sure everything's locked. We'll have a third officer in the house with you to make sure he don't get in." Huffman put his hand on her shoulder.

"Wait, you said someone will be in my house with me? You don't have to do that. He isn't in here. Detective Riggs checked himself. I think I'll be okay with just an officer at the front and back of the house." Kassidy didn't want to put a third officer at her house when there were other people in the city who may need them.

"If it's all right with you, I offered to take that job." He smiled at her for the first time since they'd met and waited for her to respond.

Kassidy knew that look on his determined face. He wanted the first crack at Tucker.

"I won't win this argument, will I?" Kassidy knew Sawyer had probably told them in no uncertain terms that her 'no' didn't matter.

"No, ma'am. Sorry, Miss Parker." Huffman moved a stool out from the island in the kitchen and planted himself on it.

"Did you need something to eat or drink?" Kassidy knew she needed to offer something after all that had happened today.

"Water would be great."

She handed the last water bottle to Huffman, who thanked her. There was another case of water in the garage and she left without a word. With case in hand, she turned around and almost screamed. Huffman towered over her at the top of the steps to the garage.

"Sorry, I wasn't sure where you was going." Huffman held out his hands to take the case of water.

"That's okay, I have it. Sorry, I didn't hear you walk up behind me." The water bottles thudded into the bottom drawer of the refrigerator as she pulled them from the partial case she'd carried in from the garage.

Her phone rang. It read Detective Riggs on the caller ID. "Hello?"

"Did Huffman give you the update?" Sawyer tried to keep the anger out of his voice.

"Yes. Please be honest. How bad is it?" Kassidy turned her back to Huffman.

"It's not good but doctors took him back for surgery right now to see what kind of damage Tucker did." Sawyer's voice was almost robotic.

"I'm so sorry this happened to him," Kassidy cried.

"Hey! You didn't do this. Remember that, Miss Parker. Tucker Miles did this, and he'll have a hard time getting anywhere near you now. There's no place he can hide in this town that we won't find him."

"I know that. It doesn't change the fact that I feel partially responsible, and you know you would too if the roles were reversed!"

"You're right. Sorry, I yelled. I'm so mad right now and I want him more than ever. He made a huge mistake today."

"I'll continue to pray for Officer Rollins. Please let me know how the surgery goes. I also have him on the church's prayer chain." Kassidy closed her eyes and moved her lips in silent prayer for the wisdom of the doctors and their ability to repair what may have been damaged when the demon inside Tucker stabbed Officer Rollins.

"Prayer chain?"

"Yes, we have a list of people who are on the prayer chain. They call the first person on the list and then they call the next person on the list and so forth. In less than five minutes you can have the whole church praying. That's what I put into action as soon as you went out to find Officer Rollins."

"Wow, I didn't know people did things like that. You did that for us?" Sawyer seemed to fight to keep his emotions in check.

"Yes, that's what we do in our church. We even pray for this town." Kassidy waited for that to sink in. She wanted to hear his response to the love her church members had for people.

"To be honest, I didn't know churches did more than just have a couple of services and Bible studies a month. But if your church does what you say it does, that sounds like one I could check out." Sawyer quietly stated.

Tears welled up in her eyes. She'd been waiting for him to say that since she'd first shared her faith with him. "Well, let me know and you can sit with me and my friends."

"I might." Sawyer didn't hesitate to utter to her. "I have to go; there's a doctor here."

She looked at the phone as he disconnected. For the first time since she'd shared her faith, she had hope that Detective Riggs would finally see what a true God-fearing church was like.

As she turned around, she saw that Huffman sat there politely as if he hadn't heard any of her conversation. "So, can I fix you guys some dinner?" Kassidy stalked to the refrigerator and pulled out numerous ingredients. Determination to feed these men took over.

Ground beef sizzled in the skillet as she diced several other ingredients for tacos. "You don't have to feed us, Miss Parker; we can have food delivered." Huffman studied her with wide eyes.

"Nope, I'm not accepting that. You guys have gone above and beyond for me and it's about time I showed you how grateful I am for it."

Kassidy grabbed several bowls for the cheese, tomatoes, lettuce, onions, sauce, and ground beef, after it was thoroughly cooked. Huffman swallowed hard then licked his lips as the appetizing aromas made his mouth water. She emptied boxes of taco shells onto a pan to heat in the oven.

"It's ready if you want to let them know." Kassidy grabbed four plates. She would eat with the men who spent so much time with her. Maybe she could get to know them a little.

Huffman walked to the back door and called the officer in as he turned on the lights. Light flooded and illuminated every inch of the yard. He smiled and walked to the front door to call the other officer in. The front lights shone bright and cast all shadows into nothingness. These were not normal lights that people had on their houses.

"Sir, do you think we should all be in the house?" Phelps looked at the front door, seeming uncomfortable that he wasn't where Sawyer wanted him.

"I think it would be rude to turn down the delicious meal this fine lady took the time to make for us. We can eat then we'll clear the outside of the house and get you guys back on post as a group. I dare Tucker to try something with all three of us in the house." Huffman motioned for Kassidy to go first.

"Oh no, I made this for you guys. Guests eat first at my house but I'll join you after you've made your plates. Please take as much as you want. I made more than enough to feed me for a week." Kassidy smiled.

"Thank you, ma'am," the officers said in unison.

They were not stingy with their taco toppings. Each officer favored certain toppings more than others as they piled double the helping on their tacos.

Kassidy took her plate and made two tacos herself and grabbed water bottles out of the freezer. Partially frozen, they squeezed the plastic bottles to knock the ice crystals down into the water. They enjoyed dinner as Kassidy asked each of them about themselves. She leaned forward and rested her elbows on the counter as each told their stories. She would never look at them the same. This was a side of them the public normally didn't get to see: a human side with so many different levels. She knew she would always pray for them now. Lights from a car pulled into the driveway and splashed the kitchen, alerting them. The officers stood, their hands automatically moving to their weapons.

Huffman was the first one to the door and waved for whoever had driven up to come on in. Sawyer climbed the stairs and raised his eyebrows at Huffman.

"Miss Parker was nice enough to make dinner for us after what happened today. I told the other two to come in we turned on all the outside lights. I figured when we finished we could check the exterior of the home together and then they could go back to their posts." Huffman took all the blame.

"Good idea. Do you have enough for another person?" Sawyer grinned at Kassidy.

"I have more than enough."

Sawyer piled the toppings on his tacos until his plate was full then dropped onto an empty stool.

The officers seated themselves back onto their stools and continued to tell Kassidy about their lives and why they chose their profession. Sawyer listened.

After Sawyer had eaten Huffman helped the two officers clear the outside of the house, before coming back in through the back door. "Sir, I hope I wasn't out of line lettin' the men come in and eat what Miss Parker fixed for dinner."

"No, it still left three officers here and clearing the outside as a group before putting them back on post was a great way to handle it."

"How's Officer Rollins?" Kassidy busied herself packing the leftovers into containers, which she then carted to the refrigerator.

"Surprisingly enough, very little damage was done. Doctors said there was a cut to his intestines but other than that, nothing vital was hit. They couldn't explain how he didn't sustain more damage. It was an easy surgery and they even said he may go home in a couple of days."

Sawyer carried the plates to the sink and stacked them for Kassidy.

Kassidy closed her eyes. "Thank you, Father."

Sawyer and Huffman looked at her when she opened her eyes. She ignored them and loaded the dishwasher.

"Well, I'll head to the station. There's a lot of paperwork to finish from tonight. Huffman, radio in if there's a problem, no matter how small it may seem. No one is to contact Tucker by themselves and she isn't to be left alone no matter what." Sawyer glanced at Kassidy, then left without another word.

Huffman walked to the back door, locked it, and gave a short salute at Officer Marks.

"So, what do I do now?" Kassidy wasn't sure how to handle an officer in her house while they searched for Tucker.

"Just go about your normal activities. I'll be in the house if you need me. Tucker may be at his breaking point with how brazen he attacked an officer today. Somethin' set him off that he's gettin' bolder and will more than likely try somethin' again. You can still have your privacy but it may upset him enough that I'm in the house with you that he'll do somethin' stupid."

Twenty-Nine

REALIZATION STRUCK with how late it was. She usually watched a movie or read her book about this time. After a glance at Huffman, she decided a movie was the polite way to go. There was a wide selection of movies she could choose from but she wasn't sure what he would like. The best option, she decided, was a black and white western.

Huffman raised his eyebrows at her when he glanced at the movie case. Quietly he grabbed a stool from the kitchen and carefully set it down in the living room. Huffman perched himself on the stool near the entry of the living room so he was at the perfect angle to see the rest of the house.

Kassidy smiled as Huffman seemed to get into the movie and even chuckled at a couple of scenes. Not sure what to do, she decided to be honest and hope he wouldn't be offended.

"I usually go to sleep about now, but please help yourself to whatever you want in the fridge. You can watch television or even sleep. There are blankets in the hall closet. Sorry, I'm not sure how this works." Heat flushed her cheeks.

"I'm fine. I'm used to the night shift rotation so I'll stay awake. I'll be here in the mornin' when you wake up." Huffman shifted his weight on the stool.

Kassidy ambled down the hall, closed then locked her door. She sunk down underneath the comforter as her head plopped onto her pillow.

Thirty

KASSIDY JUST LAY THERE and didn't want to open her eyes. She was too comfortable. She thought about what had happened over the last couple of months. How did it go from a calm, quiet life to this? She had an officer at her front door, another one at the back door and still another one in her living room.

As she sat on the edge of her bed, her legs dangled over the side. Her arm where Tucker had cut her still ached, but it wasn't as warm as it had been the other day. With a nod of her head, she knew she was past the bad part of the infection. She got up to change into her clothes to run. Hair up in a ponytail, she was ready to give her treadmill a good workout.

The stool was under the edge of the island in the kitchen when she meandered in to get water. With a wave to the officer at the bottom of the stairs outside the back door, she wondered where Huffman had gone. Water bottle in hand, it was time to see how this treadmill worked. With a deep breath, she figured she might as well get it over with. Encouraged to embrace this way to run safely—until they caught Tucker and he was in jail where he belonged—she stepped up onto the treadmill.

A shiver ran down her spine since the basement was several degrees cooler than the rest of the house. The screen intimidated her at first but with a push of a couple of buttons, she was ready to select a speed. Not sure what speeds were equivalent to how fast she normally ran, she started at a slow pace then increased it as she found her stride. The thunderous echo of the rubber soles of her shoes as they thudded on the belt with each step filled the basement.

She kept up her pace for a good forty-five minutes before she slowed down the treadmill for a cool down. Drops of sweat rolled off her and splattered onto the belt. She looked at her fitness tracker, not happy that it didn't show her step count like it did when she ran on the road with the GPS activated; she would have to figure a way to correct that.

With the treadmill turned off, she decided she could live with this if she had to. It wasn't as bad as she'd thought it would be, but she missed the sounds of nature, God's creations, at the end of her run. Maybe she could buy a CD with birds and nature sounds so she could listen to it while she ran. She decided she would look for a CD today after she'd showered and had breakfast.

A dark silhouette walking past the top of the stairs made her scream.

"Miss Parker it's me!" Huffman held up his hands and took a step back so he was in the light and not just a shadow that lurked at the top of the stairs.

"Oh, my gosh, I'm so sorry. I didn't expect anyone to be at the top of the stairs." She climbed the rest of the stairs as Huffman motioned to the officers at the front and back of the house that everything was okay.

"Wow, I have to say that was some scream."

At the top of the stairs, she turned off the light and smiled. "I'm going to jump in the shower then run an errand." The thought of a man being in her house while she showered bothered her. She locked her bedroom door and then her bathroom door too.

The steaming hot shower eased the tension out of her neck as she just stood under the spray for several moments. She was glad she could still run and that her arm didn't ache as much today. Once out of the shower, she toweled off, grabbed her robe then cinched the belt around her waist. Self-conscious, she grabbed jeans and a sweater out of her closet.

The tape on the bandages yanked hair off her arm as she pulled it off; she thought the shower would have helped loosen it. She piled on the antibacterial ointment and hoped it would help. The wound wasn't as swollen anymore, so the skin didn't pucker and push at the stitches. Maybe the scar wouldn't be too bad after it healed completely.

The braid she wove her hair into was past her shoulders again. Her hair had slowly grown back from when Tucker cut it. She flipped her braid back over her shoulder after securing it in place with an elastic hair tie.

Huffman came back into the house as she filled her bowl with cereal for breakfast. "Sorry, stepped outside until you showered. I didn't want you to feel uncomfortable or make anyone think somethin' inappropriate was going on."

"I appreciate that, thank you so much. Most people wouldn't be that considerate." Kassidy topped her cereal with milk. She held up the bowl to Officer Huffman.

"No, thanks. I'm gettin' ready to be relieved of duty; I don't eat that close to when I go to bed." Huffman's uniform was perfectly pressed. She wasn't sure if it was the material or if he had stayed awake the whole night to keep her safe.

"Thank you for staying last night. I slept better with an officer in the house." Kassidy perched on a stool as she checked her phone. Tucker had apparently tried to call several times. The name of Celeste on the caller ID made her shiver.

"What's wrong?" Huffman's eyes narrowed as he watched her.

"Tucker apparently tried to call me last night." Kassidy showed Officer Huffman her phone with the caller ID that showed Celeste's name more than a dozen times.

"But," Huffman looked at her.

"That isn't my friend Celeste. Somehow, he made his phone show her name and number when he calls. So I changed her name in my contacts to a different name so I would know when she called as opposed to him." Kassidy set down her phone to finish her cereal.

"Let me make a call; maybe there's a way to track his phone through this name and number he's usin'. Maybe we can get ahead of him for once." Huffman stepped out the back door and was on the phone before the latch clicked into the doorframe.

While she listened for the back door, she ran to her bathroom to brush her teeth. With her toothbrush placed back in its holder, she started down the hall and heard two voices coming from the kitchen. In the doorway, she spied Detective Riggs speaking with Huffman.

Sawyer smiled at Kassidy as he continued to talk. "Not sure how we can link those calls to him since it's not his real number, but I'll check into it."

"Well, I'm goin' to go home and crash. Miss Parker, have a good day." Huffman nodded to her.

"So, who's on watch today?" Kassidy was nervous about taking up so much of the police department's time.

"I am." Sawyer grinned like the cat that ate the canary.

"Wow, who did you make mad to get stuck with this detail?" Kassidy giggled.

"No one. I asked for this detail if you really want to know." Sawyer scowled at her but then the lines softened on his face.

"Well, I'll be back in a few minutes. I have an errand I want to run." Kassidy grabbed her wallet and her car keys then started for the door.

"Um, I'm afraid you don't understand. I go where you go. So, I'll keep you company on this errand you're running." Sawyer stepped in front of her at the door.

"But it's just a quick stop at a store for a CD. I can't handle running on the treadmill if I can't hear nature like I do when I run outside."

"Well then, let's go find you a CD. By the way, how was the treadmill this morning? Did it work okay?" Sawyer held the door open for her.

"Great, but I'm driving."

"Okay, I'll let you this time. But if something happens, we're switching places and I'm driving."

Sawyer climbed into the passenger seat, as Kassidy settled into the driver's seat. She headed to the only store she thought would have a nature-sounds CD. Would it sound like what she heard when she ran? There were things you couldn't replicate no matter how good the recordings were.

"You're quiet. Is everything okay?" Sawyer kept an eye on her.

"Yes, sorry I was just thinking about the CD. I hope it sounds as good as what's out there in nature." Kassidy peeked at him then looked back at the road. The heat started at her neck and crept into her cheeks. She hated that she was attracted to him and that this was how they had met—through some madman who wanted to possess her as his property. It sent a shiver through her spine.

"Are you sure?"

"That time I was thinking about Tucker."

"Well then, I can understand why you shivered. After all my years as an officer, some people still shock me. You would think I would've seen it all in this job, but I'll be honest: this is the worst case of stalking I've ever seen. Normally in situations like this, someone would've given up by now or we would've caught them. I can't explain why we're still dealing with this guy." Sawyer glanced in the side mirror and then out the back window.

"What's wrong?" Kassidy saw the muscles in his arms tense.

"I think we're being followed." Sawyer grabbed his phone to dial for officer assistance, but before he could, they were hit from behind.

Sawyer lost grip on his phone as it fell to the floor. "Drive!"

Kassidy jumped on the gas and felt the pedal touch the floor. The engine of the car caught and threw them back into their seats, locking their seatbelts. The black sedan hit them again and spun them around. Kassidy hit the gas again and figured if she could get back to her house, Sawyer would have two more officers to back him up.

The black sedan hit them a third time. They went off the road as Kassidy slammed on the brakes, but not before they broadsided a tree on the passenger side. Glass rained down on Sawyer as the window shattered. His head dropped. Blood dripped from his head where it had hit the side window on impact with the tree.

Kassidy reached to check his pulse before she tried to reach for his gun. Her driver's side window shattered as she screamed and a hand yanked her up by the hair. The seatbelt stopped her from being pulled completely from the car.

The sinister slithery voice of the possessed Tucker whispered in her ear. "Undo your seatbelt and don't say a word or I'll kill him." The large knife at her throat was more than enough motivation for her to do as he said.

Kassidy reached with her hand to push the button to release her seatbelt. Tucker yanked her through the window and she hit the ground with a thud. He hauled her up by her braid and kept her off balance as he dragged her to his car and the opened trunk. With a step back, he shouted at her to get in.

Thirty-One

KASSIDY CLIMBED AWKWARDLY into the trunk. Tucker slammed the trunk lid as tears spilled down her cheeks. Several excruciating minutes passed before she heard Tucker start the car. What was he doing in that time? Did he go back and kill Sawyer? She wasn't sure if she could live with herself if Tucker killed him because of her.

She reached to her fitness tracker and hit the start button, which illuminated the trunk so she could look for anything to defend herself with. The tracker turned off and threw her into a darkness that terrified her. She pressed the button again then started the timer for a run. Did Detective Riggs still have the app to track her with?

GROGGILY, SAWYER CAME to. He felt his head and brought down a bloody hand. It had already started to clot and was tacky on his fingers. Panic hit him when he saw that Kassidy wasn't in the driver's seat. The tree on the other side of the passenger door let him know he would have to scramble over the driver's seat to get out. His fingers brushed carpet, searching for his phone.

Finally, with his phone in hand, he pulled the tablet out of the back-seat pocket. Then he lunged over into the driver's seat and tried to start the car as he dialed the police station's officers-only line. He barked orders as the car turned over but it wouldn't pull free from the tree. He jumped out of the car, holding the side of his head as nausea hit. Steadying himself, he lumbered toward Kassidy's house. His phone rang. It was Huffman. Sawyer could hear his siren in the background through the phone and was glad that Huffman had answered the call-out since he had just left to go off duty.

Sawyer let Huffman know where he was and before he had even hung up, he could hear Huffman's siren for real. Huffman slowed down at Kassidy's car. Sawyer waved and Huffman gunned the engine then slid to a stop next to Sawyer. He yanked open the door before Huffman came to a complete stop. Once in the car, he pulled up the fitness app and waited for the GPS to pinpoint Kassidy's location.

"Where do we head?" Huffman gunned the engine and pointed the car where Sawyer told him to go. Sawyer's heart dropped: he had a feeling this time would be bad. He wasn't sure how long he'd been out to give Tucker a head start. He noticed his holster was also empty and his heart sank even further. He unlocked the shotgun and removed it from the rack.

"HELLO?" KASSIDY'S VOICE breached the metal of the trunk as Tucker turned the car off. She wished someone would hear her besides her captor.

The trunk lid opened and Tucker stood there with his trusty knife and, to her shock, a gun. Tucker saw where her eyes went and smiled to reveal teeth that looked as if they had started to decay. Tucker's skin was pale and seemed to be sloughing off his bones.

"Wakey, wakey, princess. Time to play." It looked even more malicious than the last time she remembered.

Kassidy didn't move. It lunged at her and grabbed her foot to drag her out of the trunk feet first but she fought to stay in the trunk. She wasn't sure how far behind Detective Riggs was and hoped if she could stall just a little, maybe he would get here so this would finally be over. Did he even survive the crash? She'd never seen that much blood.

Tucker screamed as she kicked and caught him in the chest with her size six shoe. He shot a round into the trunk then screeched. "Get out now!"

She tried to take her time getting out of the trunk but Tucker grabbed her by her braid and yanked her the rest of the way out. He tossed her to the ground as if she were a ragdoll. As she raised her head, all she saw were cornfields. Her heart dropped. She really hoped Detective Riggs tracked her.

Father, I need you now more than ever.

"Get up!" It yelled with such ferocity she jumped.

She didn't know what to do. Blood ran down her arm where several stitches had ripped open. A strange peace filled her and gave her hope as she slowly stood.

"Now admit it!" it screamed.

"Admit what?"

"Admit it!" Spit flew from its mouth.

Kassidy threw her arms up slightly.

"Your God isn't stronger; look who has you again." It turned in a full circle, arms out from its sides, knife in one hand, and a gun in the other.

"I'll never admit that. My God is stronger than yours! And He always will be. He's the one true God. He created everything, including you!" Kassidy yelled back.

Kassidy saw police cars crest the hill close to the clearing she was in and turn off their lights.

She smiled at Tucker. "It's not too late for you Tucker; you can still be saved."

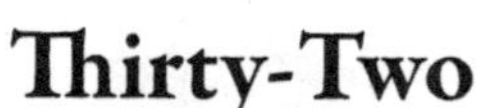

Thirty-Two

"SHE ISN'T FAR NOW; she hasn't moved for several minutes," Sawyer looked at Huffman as they approached a clearing and both saw the black sedan that had run Kassidy and Sawyer off the road. Huffman unfastened his seat belt while Sawyer unfastened his.

"Oh, Tucker's gone. He'll be mine for all of eternity. He doesn't want to be saved." It grinned as it lifted the gun and pointed it at her chest. She took a step back with her palms toward Tucker.

"My God is stronger than yours." Kassidy closed her eyes.

A shot rang out as Huffman pulled into the clearing. Half the police department of New Kingdom followed. Tucker stood there in the clearing with the gun in his hand and faced Kassidy. Miniscule particles of gun powder hung in the air.

Red spread across her chest. Her knees buckled as she fell forward.

Tucker laughed maniacally and dropped the gun. "I told you no one else would ever have her. She's mine!"

Sawyer started toward Tucker but three officers restrained him as he dragged them several inches in an attempt to get at Tucker. Huffman and another officer hit Tucker hard, as they took him down. Huffman swiveled around with his knee still on Tucker's back and stared at Kassidy's crumpled body. All the while, the laughter continued as the other officer handcuffed Tucker.

Sawyer turned toward Kassidy who was still face down. "Let me go!" he bellowed, and the officers released him. Halfway to her, he hollered back. "Get an ambulance out here now!"

Officer Huffman keyed up his portable radio and demanded medical code one response to their location.

Sawyer knelt gingerly to roll Kassidy over as she said, "My God is stronger than his."

"Just hold on, Kass. We have an ambulance on the way for you." Sawyer had never called her by her nickname before.

"It's okay; I'll be okay." She coughed as blood trickled out of her mouth and down the side of her face.

"Yes, you are. I'm staying right here. Tucker will never get out of jail. I'll make sure of it." Sawyer stuttered.

"No Sawyer, I think I'm going home." Her eyes followed the sky.

He didn't catch where she looked. "I know as soon as the doctors patch you up, I'll take you home myself."

"No." She reached up and touched his cheek as tears streamed down. "Not that home. I'm going to my Heavenly Father's house. Did you know he prepared a room just for me?"

"Don't talk like that. We can get you through this." He wept as he pulled her closer. Blood soaked the front of his clothes.

Sirens in the distance told him the ambulance would be there shortly. If Henry was on that ambulance, he would be driving faster than he should.

Sawyer saw Kassidy's eyes close. He felt for a pulse. Panic seized his chest. No, this wasn't supposed to happen. He was supposed to save her. Her arms fell lifeless at her side.

The officers all gasped as Sawyer looked up to a ray of light that illuminated Kassidy, but not from the sun—that hadn't risen yet past the cloud cover. He placed her on the ground tenderly. With a couple of steps back, he didn't know what to do. In the light, a figure in a brilliantly-white fashioned garment with a bronze sash that held a foreboding sword in a scabbard, reached his hand down and placed it over the hole in Kassidy's chest. With his other hand, he hovered over her injured arm.

A gentle voice whispered, "Not today. You're right, child: our God is stronger than his."

Kassidy inhaled deeply as her eyes opened wide. The figure offered her his hand and helped her to stand. As she stood, she was suddenly part of the same light as the male that stood there. Her hair cascaded down her back in beautiful curls and her body was whole. She wore a beautiful white gown that seemed to emit light in every direction as if millions of faceted diamonds were attached to it and reflecting the light. She was strikingly beautiful.

"Who are you?" Kassidy's voice was melodic.

"I'm Michael. Father sent me personally to heal you. He's so proud. You're to stay and be His witness to His strength and love for His children."

The light dissipated along with Michael who seemed to fade away, leaving the most amazing and awe-inspiring sunrise peeking through the heavy clouds, which seemed to clear as if God's breath blew them away.

Kassidy turned to Sawyer and smiled. He didn't remember her ever looking so beautiful. "He loves you too, Sawyer."

The light around Kassidy faded as her clothes returned to their normal earthly dullness. Blood drenched the front of her shirt from the gunshot wound that no longer existed.

Sawyer saw Henry jump out of the ambulance and grab his first-in-kit. He ran toward them as the last of the light ebbed from the Heavens. He looked toward the figure that disappeared with the light. Confusion clouded his face as he looked from Sawyer to Kassidy. It took several moments before Sawyer saw him focus on Kassidy's blood-soaked shirt. He dropped his first-in-kit and tore into it, pulling out handfuls of bandages as he knelt in front of her.

"Henry, I'm okay." Kassidy reached down for his hand to help him stand.

"Then what's this?" He motioned to her shirt

"She's okay; really she is." Sawyer finally got it.

Kassidy felt the bandage on her arm and slowly unwrapped it to reveal no wound at all. Not even a hint of the cut that she suffered at Tucker's hand.

"Wait. How's that possible?" Henry stood, jaw open, as Sawyer reached over ever so carefully and ran his hand down her smooth perfect arm.

Kassidy smiled at Sawyer while Tucker, and the demon he carried, had watched the whole event play out. There was no doubt. She was right: every knee will bow and every tongue will confess one day. Anyone who had just seen what he had, would agree. Tucker screamed.

"What was that light I saw?" Henry asked as more colors of the sunrise painted the sky.

"Michael." Kassidy smiled.

"Wait. Michael, Michael?" Henry dropped the bandages back into his kit.

"Yes, that Michael."

There was a peace that filled Sawyer. Was everything in the Bible she talked about true? He'd heard people talk about it before, but there was something more in the way she talked about it. Others always just took the parts they wanted from the Bible but she'd taken it all; said if you believe one part, you had to believe it all. It wasn't just a history book like people said it was—it was also the telling of future things to come.

He believed it all.

He bowed his head as he sunk to his knees. "Father, I don't know what to do or what to say. I know I'm a sinner and that You sent Your Son to die for me. I can't live my life without You in it anymore. Father, I pray that You come into my life. I want to give the rest of my life to You. Please forgive me for my sins and my life up to now. I ask that You come into my heart." Tears spilled down his face as he felt his personal Savior envelop him and hold him.

Kassidy knelt. Tears flowed down her cheeks as she wrapped an arm around his shoulders.

Henry walked over to place his hand on Sawyer's shoulder too and smiled. "Welcome to the family, brother."

The other officers saw this and seemed to feel the urgency to do the same. As they each dropped to their knees, they prayed and felt the resounding love of their new Heavenly Father fill them with something that was indescribable.

"My God is stronger than yours." Sawyer finally got it. He knew the truth in that statement.

As each officer accepted Christ into his heart, Tucker continued to scream as if he was being torn apart from the inside. The officers jumped up. They wrenched open the back door of the police car as it grew eerily dark at the ground where Tucker poured out of the car. He writhed in pain. The sky still showed the rising sun in the beautiful hues of pinks, purples, and oranges, but once you got below tree level, it felt cold and dark. Sawyer placed himself protectively in front of Kassidy.

Tucker screamed again as he tried to lurch back into the back of the police cruiser. Sawyer knew this wasn't natural and a voice quietly told him to be calm. He felt a peace which didn't extend to Tucker who now foamed at the mouth.

"You'll all die!" His eyes were so dark, they almost looked black. He collapsed onto the ground.

Kassidy, the officers, Sawyer, Henry, minus Josh, all said in unison. "Our God is stronger than yours."

Sawyer was sure Tucker was about to take his last breath. The darkness seemed to creep and crawl toward Tucker as if his body was absorbing it. His body contorted and broke as the demon inside fought for its hold. Sawyer heard the bones snap. A bright ray of light, brighter than the light of day, fell from Heaven and washed over Tucker's broken body so that the darkness had nowhere left to go. Sawyer heard a scream that wasn't Tucker, but came from within, as the last, smallest morsel of darkness melted into the ground.

Kassidy glanced at Sawyer who furrowed his brow.

"He's going to hell. It's dark with no light; only the eternal burning fires of hell." Kassidy looked back to the spot where the darkness had disappeared.

"Kass, who's Michael?" Sawyer didn't look at her when he asked.

"Come with me to church on Sunday and you'll find out." Kassidy smiled.

"I think I'll be there more than just Sunday."

Sawyer had fallen in love with her. It was different than anything he'd felt before. This was a pure love. He knew his life would never be the same because of this woman's love for her Heavenly Father. He had a lot to make up for, but he couldn't wait to start. With a look at his fellow officers, he knew New Kingdom would never be the same. The town was in for a new police department—one that would be devoted to the one true God.

"Our God is stronger than yours."

Don't miss out!

Visit the website below and you can sign up to receive emails whenever K. A. Moore publishes a new book. There's no charge and no obligation.

https://books2read.com/r/B-A-MAMI-UKUZ

BOOKS 2 READ

Connecting independent readers to independent writers.

About the Author

K.A. Moore, born and raised in Kansas, is a retired 911 police dispatcher with over thirteen years of service and will be the first to tell you dispatchers are a special breed all their own. Her real passion is writing and putting her imagination into works of fiction. Faith-based Christian suspense is her preferred writing theme, with wild, crazy dreams as the backdrop to many scenes that seem to come alive in her writing. As she writes, her Chihuahua scampers for the coveted position of curling up in her lap while creating her stories.

www.ingramcontent.com/pod-product-compliance
Lightning Source LLC
LaVergne TN
LVHW091040080826
845145LV00002B/569

* 9 7 8 1 9 5 7 2 2 3 1 2 4 *